Forward

"There's a fine line between danger and fun. Most of the time I can't figure out which side I'm on." – Julie Jenson

There was no way for the driver of the gold Ford Taurus to avoid the collision, even if he had seen the biker before she burst out from between two parked vans. The two men in the car had been preoccupied, absorbed in their plans for later that day. An impediment was the last thing they needed as they made their way down the quiet, tree-lined street. Being instrumental in an assassination plot planned for that evening, timing was everything. William Underwood, the U.S. Senator from Idaho, was the special guest at a dinner hosted by the President of Italy. Underwood had been contemplating a run for the White House in the next election and was currently showing interest in animal rights. Before dinner, he was expected to address a crowd at Giardino Zoologico Di Roma (Rome

Zoo) about endangered species and their rights to protection.   It was the same speech he planned to deliver in San Diego next week. He wanted to practice it before giving it in front of the U.S. media. It was there, in Rome, that the hit was arranged.

With practiced precision, the young girl leaped from her bike at the moment of impact. Auburn hair escaped from the bottom of her helmet, strands scattering in every direction. The driver slammed his foot on the break, throwing all loose items in the car flying chaotically.

The impact appeared grimmer then it actually was due in large part to the cushions hidden beneath the girl's nylon sweat suit. Knee pads containing magnets clung fast to the hood of the car. Her gloves, likewise, gripped with a magnetic hold. The aroma of burnt rubber and the crash of a mangled bike added depth to the visual depiction playing out on the narrow Roman pavement.

Squeezing her hands into fists, the magnetic bond was broken. She then rolled onto her back, released her knees' hold, and slid down the hood of the vehicle. She lay motionless on the asphalt road in front of the sedan.

Two boys darted onto the scene from between parked cars. They reached the girl at the same time the driver did.

"Julie! Are you all right?" they shouted in unison.

"Is she okay?" the driver questioned. "I didn't see her, really."

Julie moved her head and gradually lifted it. "What happened?" she inquired.

"What's going on out there?" a ruff voice barked. Out of the car stepped a tall man in a black suit. "We don't have time for this, Ed," he yelled, keeping one leg in the car as he leaned on the open door. "Get in!"

"But our friend has just been hit," the red-haired boy pleaded.

The man could now see the top of Julie's blue and yellow helmet over the front of the car as she gingerly sat up. "Is the girl alright, Ed?" he said in a feigned sincere voice. This was absolutely the last thing they needed. If the police were brought in, the entire scheme would go bust. *I have to get rid of these kids,* he thought. Ed nodded his return.

Julie pushed herself to her feet. Slightly wobbly, she rubbed the back of her neck and the small of her back, both to hide the magnetic gloves and because they ached from the impact.

"She looks fine to me," the willowy impatient man said, pointing to Julie with an open hand.

"Her bike is completely destroyed, Mister," the shorter boy argued, glancing down at the mauled bicycle.

The bike, thought the man. He could not leave it behind. It would be tangible evidence to support the kid's story if they went to the police.

While the two men's eyes remained fixed on the bike, the taller boy reached inside his pocket and pressed a button on a small unit no bigger than a car door remote. In the distance, the familiar high pitch-low pitch of a police car siren resonated and gradually grew louder. The well-dressed, edgy man turned toward the sound. A dreaded look creased his forehead for a moment and quickly vanished.

"Look," the man said hurriedly. "Here's some cash for a new bike, and buy yourself ice cream or something. We'll take this old bike and get rid of it for you." He handed the fair, shorter boy a wad of bills and instructed Ed to pick up the pieces of the bike, quickly. "I'm really sorry, but we're late for a meeting."

As soon as the street was spotless, the men hastily climbed back in the auto and sped away from the sound of the approaching sirens.

"All right, Connor. You can turn off the sirens," Julie Jenson told him, pulling the gloves from her hands. "That hurt more than practice did. I think he was speeding." She removed her helmet and pushed loose locks away from her face. The remainder of her wavy hair fell down her back.

"Speeding will be the last crime they get away with," Doug Winslow presumed, eyeing the direction the car fled.

The three friends moved from the quiet street.

Julie stopped when she got to the sidewalk. "Hey, how come you guys acted more concerned with the bike and not me back there?" she asked with mock sarcasm.

"Because we know your head is as hard as a rock, Julie. So there was no reason to worry about you," Connor O'Farrell said laughing. Connor's red hair appeared almost brown, seeing as he wore it in a crew cut. He in no way liked the color and found that the shorter hair length left less hair to be conspicuous. His sister Molly, on the other hand, loved the color of her crimson hair.

"That's right, Red," Doug said, circling his arm around Julie's shoulder. The two were both twelve and roughly the same height. Doug and Julie had grown closer over the last year and enjoyed each other's wit and sarcasm. They had worked together on school projects for the past two years and grew quite accustomed to one another. Connor, conversely, was new to their team, but had a great deal more experience then either of his new partners. He was assigned to work with them a couple of months ago. Being fourteen, they jokingly referred to him as their chaperon.

"Hey guys, look at this," Doug said, holding out the money the man had given to him. "There's six hundred Euros here."

"Wow!" Connor exclaimed. "That's a perk to the job."

"How about a late lunch?" Julie asked, still massaging a sore spot in the middle of her back. "Or maybe a shopping spree here in Italy?"

"Sounds good—the eating part, that is. If we're talking food, I'm paying," Doug announced, waving the money above his head.

The three enjoyed the laugh for a moment.

"Doug, you get the sound unit. I'll call Mr. McMichael," Connor instructed, returning the group back to business.

Doug shoved the money into his front pocket and headed down the sidewalk toward a thicket of bushes.

Connor pulled out a rectangular device, pressed a button, and waited. A voice instructed him to enter his pass code. Connor moved the unit from his ear and pressed his code, then resumed listening.

In a matter of moments, he heard a familiar voice.

"Connor, this is Mr. McMichael. How did things go?"

Connor pictured Mr. McMichael sitting in his wheelchair behind the large oak desk in his office. It was never clear as to what events put him into the wheelchair. No one talked about it or dared ask. The students at Wesley-Hampton Academy, the school they attended, had their own theories. Some thought it happened during a clandestine government job. It was not a secret that Mr. McMichael once worked for the CIA before he became their headmaster. Others speculated it was an accident on one of his dangerous ventures. He was known to have climbed mountains, scuba dived, and was a spelunker in his free time. Although he did not have a theory of his own, Connor did not side with either faction. He never felt compelled to figure it out.

"We just finished. Operation 'Dog Leg' was..." he looked at Julie. She nodded. "A success. The unit is in place."

"Wonderful! Great Job! Kudos to your team, Connor." Connor thanked him for the accolades. "Did anything happen that we didn't prepare for?"

How does he always know when something out of the ordinary happens? Connor asked himself.

"Actually, yes," he confessed. "We were given six hundred Euros for the bike."

There was a pause. "That sounds like Hamilton; tall guy, impatient. Why don't you three get something to eat and bring in the rest when you get back to the states?"

Connor acknowledged the idea and assured Mr. McMichael he would e-mail his report when they got back to the hotel. He returned the communication device back inside his pocket.

Doug approached them with a small green box in his hand. "Did you get through to McM?" he asked in cavalier voice.

"Yeah," Connor said. "No further jobs. Just return to the States." He paused briefly. "Why us? Why have we only been given set-up roles recently? Put a trace unit under the bumper of a car," he continued, not giving anyone else a chance to talk. "Team Three is going to finish this and get all the credit. It's not fair."

"Look, Connor, we work as a team. We haven't gotten the great jobs recently. I'm sure it's nothing," Doug responded. He heard all this before. Connor was his roommate back at school and both being on Team Two, he had to admit he felt a little slighted also.

Feeling the tension, Julie quickly interrupted, "Let's eat!"

They agreed on someplace familiar and decided on McDonald's. The atmosphere was similar to back home, but the food tasted a little different.

Connor chewed a bite from his chicken sandwich with a blank stare. "It's just not right. Mr. McMichael has not given us any good assignments. It's like he doesn't trust us."

"I think you're reading too much into it," Julie said, aiming a french fry at him.

"I don't think so," Connor disagreed. "Somewhere out there Team Three is preparing to spring the trap and catch those guys in the act." He picked up a fry and began turning it in ketchup.

"Look," Doug started, "we're shorthanded. When we get a bigger team I'm sure we'll get a bigger piece of the pie, Connor."

"Doug's right," Julie chimed in. "Wait until the new kids arrive."

"New kids!" Connor snorted. "One of those new kids is my sister Molly. Mr. McMichael is sure to put her on our team."

"I'm sure she'll do just fine," Julie assured him.

"Maybe, but we'll have to start the training from the beginning. Team Two will never be the top team again."

A hush fell over them as the trio finished their meals and headed back to the hotel to pack. Though doubts rolled around in their minds, the adventure was only beginning.

Chapter One
"When things look good, something somewhere must look bad." – Matt Malone

The outward appearance of 421 Sycamore made most passersby envious. The vibrant gardens and lawn were impeccable. The wraparound porch showed not a hint of ageing and the painted siding was never chipped or faded. It was, without argument, the most stunning house on the street.

That was the external appearance; the inward was seen by only a few. 421 Sycamore in truth was a well-shrouded prison for eight young boys ranging in ages from six to fourteen. It was the foster home for ill-fated children, run by a middle-aged women using every angle dreamed up to make money from the state at the expense of childhood. The fraud was well-rehearsed and polished to perfection. Over the years, fourteen social workers had inspected the house and found it fit and safe for children. Never had any one of the state's servants exposed harsh treatment or unsafe environments for the guest occupants. On the contrary, each report indicated a welcoming, engaging environment for the youngsters. After all, the children were surrounded by ample activities to participate in. One room was told to be the favorite; it was filled with shelves of books and puzzles, games and music CDs. Soft comfortable sofas and beanbags dotted the floor, and several tables displayed partially finished puzzles.

It appeared the perfect place to be, if it had been all real. None of the fourteen social workers ever compared their notes or reports. If they had, there would have been a number of questions and raised eyebrows. On all fourteen reports spread over the past six years the daily menu in the kitchen was dutifully observed, but it was never to be noticed that the observations were identical for one reason—the list never changed. It consisted of the same meals everyday without exceptions.

Breakfast: Cereal of your choice
   (one choice: generic corn flakes)
Toast
Milk (made from powder)
Fruit (one banana divided equally)
Lunch: Sandwich of the day (always
   peanut butter, no jelly)
Tomato soup (made with ketchup and water)
Milk
Fruit (one apple divided equally)

Dinner: Pasta Surprise (canned
    ravioli, unheated)
Vegetable platter (celery stalk on a plate)
Milk
Fruit cup (one grape and one
    cherry in a cup)

The bedrooms were described in one social worker's report as "any child's dream bedroom." Each of the four rooms housed a bunk bed, two dressers, a desk for homework, and a television hooked up to two of the latest video systems accompanied with countless games. The walls were painted cheerfully and tastefully, emulating a warm and welcoming feeling. The reports claimed the bedrooms to be in perfect condition with everything picked up and not a sock out of place. If anyone looked closer, the person would have discovered there were no socks or underwear to begin with. The drawers were empty, the bed had comforters but no sheets, and even the televisions were empty shells.

And on and on it went. Everything was a charade, a clever cover over the real workings of 421 Sycamore. Only the eight boys and Mrs. Helmut knew the entire truth and it seemed that was the way it was to remain . . . until one particular rainy day in August.

The rain came down as if fire hoses were being shot from the sky. The sound of the torrential water made it difficult to hear conversations in the attic deep within the pompous manor. Three boys lay silently on mattresses strewn across the floor of the grimy room. Grubby clothes piled in a corner of the room, with soiled knees and filthy armpits, waited for laundry day. The only light shone from a single bulb hanging with a carefree sway from the peaked roof.

"Does anyone know where Matt is?" the youngest of the eight asked, nearly yelling to be heard.

"He's probably in the basement, Joey. I think that's where he goes," a larger boy answered, not breaking his stare at the bulb.

Joey stood up and walked to the door. His clothes hung on his withered frame of a body. It was apparent that nothing he wore was his actual size.

"Be careful!" the larger boy warned as Joey left the room.

Getting around the house was difficult, if not dangerous, when Mrs. Helmut's whereabouts were unknown. If she found you wandering around the house the punishment could be painful. Joey, in the two years he lived there, had been slapped, spanked, fed Tabasco sauce, and kicked more than once. Tim, the eldest child, shared similar horrid stories of a previous foster boy getting his arm broken in two places for talking to one of the social workers without Mrs. Helmut present. No one knew if the story was true or not, but no one wanted to find out firsthand.

Joey descended the stairs leading to the second floor and tiptoed down the hallway. Mrs. Helmut was not known to spend much time in the rooms upstairs. She was oddly fond of the kitchen, but did not cook. Another favorite location for her was the master bedroom on the first floor. When she was not in either of those two places one never knew where she'd pop up. The boys were allowed in the rooms on the second floor only for dusting. It was the children's responsibility to keep them clean. The younger ones usually were assigned as dusters and cleaners.

Joey safely arrived at the top of the stairs looking down the enclosed stairway, listening for clues of Mrs. Helmut's presence. If it had been a Sunday, she might have been at the kitchen table planning jobs for the week, jobs the boys looked forward to.

Work was the most welcomed event at 421 Sycamore. With the exception of Sunday, the boys were farmed out in the neighborhood to clean, rake, weed, paint, or attend to any other task requested by the neighbors. The employers would pay well for the boy's sweat and brawn, and Mrs. Helmut, who hadn't lifted a finger to work in ages, would collect. She would tell Mrs. Brown at the end of the block, "The boys need new clothes this week," and Mrs. Brown would happily pay twice the price for the work. While filling her heart with satisfaction, she filled Mrs. Helmut's purse with cash.

The small brown-haired boy stealthily made it to the bottom of the stairs. Joey still had a ways to go to get from the stairs to the door off the kitchen that led to the cellar. He prayed his footsteps wouldn't give him away, and with ten more feet to go his heart banged against his ribs with excitement. But it was the bang of the thunder that stopped his heart, and he was caught breathless, frozen in his footsteps. When he regained his heartbeat and oxygen intake, he took a cautious step forward as if the atmospheric crash disclosed his location. As he crossed the floor, a glimpse of light reflected off a jar purposely placed on a small table in the corner. Of course, the jar was empty—again.

Sometimes customers paid and then provided an additional tip for the boys working the job. This money had to be added to the "Turn-in Jar." The jar was an old pickle jar that never held the money long. No one knew where the money went. It certainly wasn't being worn, eaten, or enjoyed by the boys at 421 Sycamore. Mrs. Helmut probably squirreled it away for her own enjoyment and the boys could only guess what that was. If your tip didn't make it to the jar and it was discovered you were in mortal danger.

Last year Patrick, an older boy, held onto his money and neglected to turn it in. It was his money, he rationalized. He worked for it. One night when Mrs. Helmut found his stash behind a loose board in the attic, she had Patrick follow her downstairs. The beating seemed to last for hours. He didn't return for three days. Where he was for those days and nights was still unclear, but when he returned he was covered in bruises and a few lacerations. Three more days went by before Patrick even talked about it. He told them he didn't know where he was for those three days. He didn't even know three days had passed. Without light, it was impossible to determine the time of day. Food was left in the room when he roused. On the last day, he woke up on the floor of the kitchen. Mrs. Helmut told him if it happened again he might regret where he woke up. This story always sent shivers through each boy.

Joey finally reached the door to the basement. The trick, he knew, was to open the door without making a sound. Slowly he turned the round doorknob and gently pulled back. It opened smooth and quiet, until the rusting hinges let out a loud screech of pain, and the wider he opened the door the louder and longer the hinges screamed. Like a mouse in middle of the kitchen floor stunned by a light being turned on and its position completely compromised,

Joey froze solid and listened for the sounds that were guaranteed to be heard next: the hasty, heavy footsteps of Mrs. Helmut. However, an unexpected sound preceded the anticipated noise: the doorbell rang.

"Oh, for the love of—!" Mrs. Helmut screamed above the sound of the hinges, the rain, and Joey's heart. He listened to her footsteps move toward the door and, without waiting another second, he slipped past the door and quickly, quietly scuttled down the stairs.

No sooner did he reach the bottom step than his arm was almost wrenched from its socket. He wanted to scream in agony but a hand was quickly secured over his mouth.

"This way," a familiar voice instructed in a whisper, and a force pulled Joey away from the stairs.

The basement was dark, but two small windows provided enough light from outdoors to see. Joey could tell he was being dragged toward the far side of the damp and musty cellar, toward the furnace.

The guide moved open a large air return vent without making the slightest sound and the two slipped into the furnace as the thud of the basement door echoed far behind them.

Inside the completely dark cavern, the two boys waited for the new storm to arrive with its own thunder. They sat on the remarkably clean floor of the hollowed and unused heating system as light from the now illuminated basement swept in through small holes and seams.   They were motionless as they listened.

"I know you're down here, you little scum crumb! There's no use in hiding. I'll find you! And when I do…" There was a loud crash as a kicked box landed on top of a table full of gardening supplies.

The search lasted for nearly five minutes and more boxes were kicked or thrown until the sound of the doorbell could be heard ringing again.

"I'll be back!" Mrs. Helmut yelled as she raced up the stairs, slamming the door and leaving the room dark.

"Wow! That was close," Joey hoarsely whispered.

"Oh, I've seen it closer," Matt Malone told him as he pressed a button and lights came on in the little room.

Joey was stunned. He had never been in Matt's hideout; in fact, he didn't even know Matt had one. All the boys wondered where Matt disappeared to during free time. They only knew that Mrs. Helmut didn't know either.

Joey looked around and was amazed at what he saw. On one side of the furnace interior was a map of the entire house at 421 Sycamore with red and blue lines drawn over it. The opposite wall was covered in buttons and switches. Most had labels: hall light, downstairs bedroom, living room light, upstairs hall light, kitchen radio, and bathroom radio.

Joey stared at the labels for a moment and then looked at Matt. "You're the reason for the strange things in the house." Matt only smiled. "But how?"

"Are you asking the magician to give away his secrets?"

Joey nodded.

"About a year ago I discovered the reason we never had heat in the house." He waved his hand around. "This furnace was empty. So I began using it as a refuge from Helmut. I worked the return vent for my entrance until it swung quietly and I had the perfect hideout."

"Wow," Joey gasped. "That's incredible!"

"When I found this place it had more wire than I could use and I found all the switches in the TVs and games," the brown-haired boy explained. "The wiring all comes down to the basement and I was able to tap into it. I ran the wire into nearby ducts and wired it all right there," he said, pointing to the makeshift cardboard panel.

"What's that button there do?" Joey asked, admiring a small button at the top.

"Oh, that's my 'Hectic Helmut' button, I call it. It makes the doorbell ring." Matt smiled mischievously. "It's my favorite."

Joey looked from the button to Matt. "You made the bell ring when I was coming down here, didn't you?"

Matt grinned wider. "I heard the door open. I knew it wasn't Helmut. She never opens the door slowly. I knew it had to be one of us."

Joey sat back, feasted his eyes on the controls, and sighed. "Do you think we'll ever get out of here, Matt?"

Matt gently placed his hand on Joey's bony shoulder. "Someday, Joey, we'll get out of here, and when we do it will be the best day of our lives."

"I wonder what will happen to me when I get out. I'm nowhere near as smart as you are, Matt. You're smarter than anyone in here; even Mrs. Helmut, I bet."

"Don't put yourself down, Joey. You're a smart kid. Don't think differently. Besides, it doesn't take much to be smarter than Helmut. She thinks she's pretty clever. Let me show you something."

Matt pulled a shoebox down from one of the cold air ducts at the top of the furnace. It was full of paperback books and paper. He quickly rifled through the box for one particular sheet. Joey began asking him questions about the books, which were not allowed in the house.

"They are from Mr. Clifton's electronics store. He lets me have them when I garden at his house," Matt went onto explain to Joey as he held the document he was searching for. "Mr. Clifton knows we are not to accept anything from our customers other than payment. But he knows I love electronics so he gives me these books to read. I get them into the house by hiding them. Sometimes I will put them in a bag of dirt or at the bottom of the weed basket that we bring back to dump for compost. Helmut never searches those things. When I store them in the garage I slip them in the vent and they slide right down here."

"How many books do you have?"

"I guess around fifty, maybe more. They're mostly about electronics, computer repair, and circuitry. I've learned a lot from them. Which leads me to this…" he said, displaying the flyer for Joey.

"Several weeks ago Mr. Clifton and I were talking about advances in magnetic fields and power cell research when he handed me that," Matt said, tapping the colorful paper in Joey's hand.

Joey stared at Matt for a moment wondering how smart his friend really was and then looked down at the paper.

He read aloud from the flyer: "Wesley-Hampton Academy; Boston, Massachusetts. Boys and girls ages 8–17. Apply today." He looked up. "You didn't. Did you?"

"At first I didn't want to, but Mr. Clifton convinced me to try. I filled out the application and wrote a letter telling more about me. I talked about being a foster child and working all the time."

"Did you talk about Mrs. Helmut?"

Matt shook his head no. "If it got back that I wrote anything … I do have some fears," he admitted with a shrug. "Mr. Clifton told me he would send it out and use his home address. He also included a letter that he didn't let me read." Matt took the paper back and returned it to the book. "I haven't heard anything since. I'm not surprised."

Footsteps upstairs resonated through the ceiling beams, moving quickly to the front door, and the doorbell rang again. Matt held up his hands and declared, "Not my doing." The boys exchanged a curious glance, both wondering the same thing.

Chapter Two
"One must only be more prepared then her opponent."
– Molly O'Farrell

Sunlight shone in from the window next to the bed. It warmed and illuminated the surface of the dresser across the room. Very little of the sun's light actually touched the surface; there was only a small area not covered with memorabilia. Most of the light danced above the dresser's top as it reflected, bent, and glistened on the twelve trophies on display. The sun had already highlighted the others that relaxed on a shelf against the opposite wall. The visiting beams had never seen the five that were too large for shelves or dresser. Each of these displayed awards had two things in common: they were martial arts honors and they were all first place. There were several judo, a few kabuto, a couple aikido tributes, but most of them (including the largest) were karate.

Molly O'Farrell had been studying martial arts for the past eight years. Starting at the tender age of three, the routine was part of the daycare she attended. Her mother, in those eight years, had moved up through the ranks speedily as a real estate agent. She kept her den as her daughter kept her bedroom: full of acclimates. Plaques covered the walls. Mrs. O'Farrell hung every award she had ever received. It wasn't long before the picture of she and her two children was lost in a sea of wood and brass. Susan O'Farrell's motto was "sell Tacoma," and she held to it. For the past six years, she was the number one agent in all of the Sea/Tac area, and it was never by a small margin. That same tenacity coursed through the blood of her children.

Connor was the oldest child in the family and loved to read almost as much as he loved math. Words and numbers were his specialty. By the time he was ten he could speak German and Spanish, and enough Italian to hold a conversation. By that same year, he was taking an Algebra II class at the high school. When he turned twelve, his mother received a call from the Wesley-Hampton Academy. They were highly interested in Connor's talents. Everything sounded great to Connor; he had often wished to see the other coast. His mother was partial to the offer of scholarship money and the simple fact that someone else would be spending time watching her son. It was not that Susan didn't like her children, but rather a promise she made to herself when her husband impetuously left with his young intern at the pharmacy. She vowed then and there to embark upon a career of her own, provide everything her children wanted, and never, ever look back.

The offer from Wesley-Hampton Academy fulfilled her wish for Connor. If he wanted to move so far from home and pursue his dream, she was not going to hold him back. During the talk at dinner that night, she blessed his choice. The blessing was enough fuel for Molly's own argument two years later when her telephone call came.

She sat quietly on the edge of the bed looking at the letter of acceptance she had set to memory weeks earlier. The day she awaited finally arrived. All her things were packed into a single duffle style bag. The only thing left to do was wait.

Molly's mom franticly scribbled on a piece of paper on the kitchen counter and then began thumbing through a thick soft covered book. "No, they can't do that," she said for the third time. "Here, I found it! I'm going to fax this over to you right now!"

Susan listened for a moment to the caller and said, "I don't think that will make a difference. I'm leaving for the airport with my daughter in ten minutes. I could drop it off on the way." There was a listening pause. "If that's the only way it will work, then fine. I

Howell, MR.   Wesley-Hampton Academy

will be over to the title and bond building in fifteen minutes."

They exchanged valedictions and she hung up.

"Molly! We're leaving. Right now!" she called out to her daughter. "I'll be in the car."

Molly threw her bag in the back seat of the Land Rover and climbed in the front. "What's the rush, Mom?"

Backing out of the drive, Mrs. O'Farrell explained while looking from one mirror to another. "Oh, Herman needs me to talk to some people about some land. It's a zoning issue. They want a different zone for the land so they can..."

Molly had already tuned out the explanation as soon real estate became the topic. In the matter of a few hours, she would be initiated into Wesley-Hampton Academy. Her dreams came true. She had talked a little with her brother about school, but he was always tight-lipped. He never told her much. Most of the communication was done via e-mail. It was in one of the letters that Connor had sent her that opened the door for more communication. Not more correspondence with her brother, but rather her brother's friend, Beth. In a rather dull letter, Connor wrote that he would be in Dallas for a class assignment over the next two weeks. Molly almost pressed delete after she read it until she

The Weatherman   Page 29

noticed   it   copied   another   e-mail   address: clovene@wha.org. The recipient ended up being Beth (Elizabeth) Cloven.   She immediately typed a letter to Beth and their furtive correspondence began.

Over the next year, Molly and Beth wrote each other several times a week. The secret was kept completely from Connor. Beth understood the privacy rules at Wesley-Hampton Academy. The students were not to talk about the daily happenings to anyone outside the academy.   When letters were written home, the students followed strict guidelines, talking only about the mainstream academic courses.   Travel abroad or domestic was referred to as "field trips" and they were at the school's expense. Each parent completed a form for travel and the rest was in the hands of the school, no questions asked.

On the surface, Wesley-Hampton Academy was a wonderful place for any child. It offered state-of-the-art learning and plenty of travel experience. Every student was completely happy and enjoyed their time there.   On days when parent visits were planned, everything appeared picture perfect.

Molly had never been to the school and had no reason to doubt Beth and her letters.   The information was tantalizing. When her brother was home last Christmas for break, Molly absorbed a few subtle hints. She would catch him mid-sentence with a question, and occasionally drew bits and pieces of information from him, thus convincing her that the facts were real. Beth's credibility passed the test.

The SUV pulled up to the curb of the Seattle-Tacoma International Airport. Molly sat and waited for her warm goodbye, but her mother did not get out. "Are we going to park in the lot, Mom?"

"Molly, I swear you don't listen to me. I explained all the way over here that I have a meeting," her mother explained, exasperated. "I'm dropping you off. I'm sorry."

Molly looked at her a moment and said, "That's fine, Mom. I'll be okay." She opened her door and stepped out. Susan did the same. They met on the sidewalk. Molly held her bag tightly.

"Are you sure you're alright, sweetheart?" Molly knew something was bothering her mom. She never called her sweetheart unless she felt guilty about something.

"I'm fine, Mom. All I have to do is get on the plane and then I'm off. Someone will be at the airport from the school to pick me up."

Susan gave her daughter a look of sincerity and kissed her on the cheek. "Please call me when you get settled in. You hear me?"

"Yes, Mom. I will." She kissed her mother back. A part of Molly wanted to run into the airport and jump onto the plane. Another part yearned to wrap her arms around her mom and not let go.

Mrs. O'Farrell glanced down at her watch. "I have to go, sweetheart. You be good and study. I want to hear great things from you."

A final hug and she was back in her Land Rover and gone. Molly walked into the airport behind a family talking about heading to Disney World. She wondered if family life as she knew it was now over.

Chapter Three
"Freedom is just another word for good-bye."
– Joey Samson

Matt and Joey listened as footsteps crossed above them. There were several different sets and a strange sound. It sounded like pressure, but not the kind a foot would produce.

"Who do you think they are?" Joey asked as if Matt would give him the correct answer.

Matt listened a moment longer. "I don't know for sure. It sounds like there are four, plus Helmut. They're heading toward the kitchen," he explained. Matt slid over in front of Joey and pulled out a pair of black headphones from behind the cardboard panel of buttons. He plugged them into a jack labeled "kitchen" and switched something on. For nearly a minute, he listened quietly while his partner kept asking him to tell him what was going on.

Finally, Matt took off the headphones and turned to Joey. "It's the people from Wesley-Hampton

Academy! They're here to talk to Helmut." Before Joey could say anything Matt turned away and positioned the headphones back on his head.

Several anxious minutes passed before Matt finally took off the headphones. He turned and looked at Joey and smiled. "I'm in!" he exclaimed.

"You're in the school?" Joey asked.

Matt nodded his head. "That's not all. They're taking me with them. Today!"

Joey's lower jaw dropped as he stared at Matt. "How can they do that? Are you being adopted?"

"I don't know, Joey, but I know I need to be walking through that kitchen about now," said Matt moving toward the duct door.

Joey grabbed his arm and stopped him. "Matt, how can they just walk in here and take you? What about the rest of us?" Joey asked, a tear forming in his brown eyes.

"Joey, if I could take you I would. You know that. But I don't want to be here anymore than you do," Matt told him not wanting to see his best friend cry. "But this is my chance to escape this dump. I promise I will tell someone about Helmut. Someone that will act quickly so none of you guys gets hurt in her wrath." Matt watched the tear slide down the young boy's face and felt a couple forming in his own green eyes.

He pushed open the door to the hideout and looked back at Joey. "This place is yours now. Take care of it, will you?"

Joey nodded. He grabbed Matt's arm. "Are you sure you're making the right decision, Matt?"

"I'm not sure of much right now, Joey. I hope I am."

"I'm coming upstairs with you," he said, wiping a wet smear across his cheek.

The two boys reached the top of the stairs without another word. Matt reached for the doorknob and held it for a moment. *This is it,* he thought. Was it for real or would Helmut find some way to send the men away? If she did, he would pay for it with pain. Moreover, he imagined Mrs. Helmut enjoying every minute of it.

One last long breath and he opened the door.

The duo walked from the basement door to the kitchen. Matt surveyed the scene as they casually entered the room. There was Mrs. Helmut, anger forming in the creases of her face as she sat at the table. Two out of the ordinary men in suits, writing on pads of papers and rifling through files in their briefcases, sat across from Mrs. Helmut. Everyone was in a kitchen chair except one man. He wore a dark blue turtleneck shirt that bulged at the sleeves, and he sat in a wheelchair. This man was strong, Matt realized, and he had an air of leadership. He watched as one of the men handed the boss-like man a paper.

"Here it is, Mr. McMichael."

"Thank you, Kurt," he said, accepting the paper. "According to this I now have legal guardianship of the young boy."

"That stupid piece of paper is not going to take anyone out of here," Mrs. Helmut spat.

They all looked at the two boys standing in the doorway. No one spoke at first, until Mrs. Helmut broke the silence. "What are you two boys doing down here?" she snarled and then caught herself. "I mean, why aren't you playing upstairs with the other boys?"

Matt didn't want to pass up a perfect opportunity. He entered the room and walked toward the refrigerator. "I was just getting a little hungry and thought I would grab a bite before supper. Joey just wanted to come along." He glanced behind himself and noticed Joey was still frozen in the doorway, obviously timid of stepping anywhere in the room.

"I don't want you boys to be eating between meals, now," she said in her sweetest and most compassionate voice. Matt could tell it was killing her to be this pleasurable. "Go upstairs and play one of your game systems, boys."

Matt reached his hand on the icebox door and waited a moment. "Alright," he said in a singsong way. "You sure are a meanie." He could swear he heard a slow exhale of breath coming from his nemesis. If he did, it was only for a moment because there was no breathing after what he thought would be his finest moment. It would be something for his immortality, for the guys to talk about him after he was gone.

Matt pulled open the door and said, "I'll just get a glass of juice and be on my way."

The door swung open and revealed its truth. "Looks like we need more juice," Matt announced. "Oh! And the light's burned out, too."

Everyone in the room peered at the empty refrigerator, except Mrs. Helmut. She jumped out of her chair and raced over and closed the door. "You're going to let out all the cold air. Now run along, Matt," she instructed, grabbing his forearm as hard as she could. He could feel her nails pierce his flesh.

"I don't believe there is much cold air coming from that empty appliance," a voice interrupted.

Matt and Mrs. Helmut turned to look at Mr. McMichael. "It is not running. Very little in this house is," he said looking up from a small device the size of a PDA.

"I don't know what you're talking about," Mrs. Helmut stammered. "I'm going to call the police if you do not leave." She released her death grip on Matt and moved toward the telephone on the wall.

"Please do, Mrs. Helmut. It will speed things up around here," Mr. McMichael pressed her with complete composure.

"It will speed up your leaving," she shot back.

"Be my guest," he reiterated. "When they arrive we can give them a tour of this magnificent foster home you have here."

She looked at the man in the wheelchair. His unblinking blue eyes were locked on hers. "I don't know what you're talking about," she snarled, still holding the undialed phone.

Mr. McMichael turned to one of the other men in the room and said something only they could hear. Immediately the men retrieved a file and handed it to him. Mr. McMichael opened the file. "Let's start with the social worker's reports, shall we."

Mrs. Helmut set the receiver in its cradle and stood there looking at him with a grimace on her face.

"Each of these reports speaks of televisions for the children. I'm not seeing any TVs for the boys. The only one I can see is the one in your bedroom," he began, looking again at his PDA-like gadget. "How do you explain this?"

"I don't have to explain anything to you or your cronies," she screamed, her spittle traveling across the room. "You can't tell squat from that thing. You're just trying to scare me. Well, it's not going to work."

"Maybe I am bluffing. Maybe I don't have a clue to what's happening around here. Maybe I should just pack up and go," he paused, his blue eyes locked again on Mrs. Helmut. "Or maybe you should return to this table and discuss the release of this boy," he said, pointing to Matt.

For the first time in several minutes, Matt was no longer the fly on the wall. He was pulled into something that was much bigger then himself. Suddenly he lost that cavalier feeling and felt all his knowledge and skills vanish. This guy in the wheelchair was for real and nothing scared him. He was completely unnerved by Helmut and she was cracking fast. For years he had seen her talk and wiggle her way out of every situation. In a far-off way, he envied her ability to manipulate people and get everything to work out in her favor. Mr. McMichael stroked his graying, trim beard.

"There is nothing you can say or do that would make me sign over the boy," Mrs. Helmut told him in a suddenly calm voice.

Matt wondered if she was beginning to see this man in the same light as he was. He watched as

Mrs. Helmut moved across the room and leaned herself against the counter.

"Before we leave here today, you will sign these papers," Mr. McMichael said with a smile. "They are official forms signed by the governor here in Florida."

"They could be signed by Mickey Mouse, but I am not signing," she injected with a surge of energy.

"Very well," he said, reaching over his shoulder as the man named Kurt handed him a file almost on cue. Opening the folder he said, "Let us see what we have here … It looks like you have been very busy, Mrs. Helmut. You have quite a trail of money from this house," he said and looked up at her. "Does the IRS know about it?"

All the eyes in the room jumped from Mr. McMicheal's proclamation to Mrs. Helmut. When the word "IRS" reached her ear, every muscle in her legs gave out and she began to fall to the ground. Catching herself, she pulled upright with the help of the counter.

"From my information, you have been a naughty girl. Does the name Dunston Labs sound familiar? They received, to date, $1,130,450.32 over the past twelve years," he said with no show of emotion. "I could continue if you would like. I have more."

Had Mrs. Helmut held any strategic edge in this entire visit, it was completely gone. Everything from state checks to money from odd jobs around the neighborhood to late night counting and filling out deposit slips for a bank in Topeka—it all flashed through her mind. She knew a day of reckoning might come around, but this was not what she expected. If these people were from the government, what did they want with the release of the boy? What if she simply signed the papers? Would they quietly leave and not ask any questions? Something didn't make sense. Maybe she still had a chance to come out of this without it all falling apart. She walked to the table with her legs still weak. "What do you say we start all over again, Mr. McMichael, wasn't it? My name is Harriet." She held out her hand.

Mr. McMichael ignored her gesture. He was growing tired of this visit and wanted to return to Boston as soon as possible. "Let me be frank with you, Mrs. Helmut—"

"Harriet."

"Harriet," he corrected. "I am not with the government." He watched her tilt her head slightly as she tried to sort out the last fact. "I am the headmaster of a prep school in Massachusetts. It's just outside of Boston. I received a letter from Matthew Malone stating his interest in attending Wesley-

Howell, MR.   Wesley-Hampton Academy

Hampton Academy. We did the background work and followed up on his reference, a Mr. Sid Clifton. We were very impressed." He paused.

"There was only one problem. Our search was not a conventional background search. When we put your name in the computer, it made a very curious connection. I must ask you again: do you know about Dunston Labs?"

Mrs. Helmut stared at Mr. McMicheal's calming blue eyes and said, "I don't know of a Dunston Labs, but I do know a Raymond Dunston. He was my sister Patty's husband. He came to me after her death." The words began to come easier for her the more she explained. "He's not a decent man. The police investigated her death. They had determined it was murder. Somehow evidence was discovered at the scene that implied me—" She stopped. She put her face down into her hands.

Mr. McMichael rolled over to a countertop and returned with a box of tissues. He pulled a few out and handed them to her.

For the first time, Matt felt sorry for Mrs. Helmut. He didn't know how the story was going to play out or even if Mrs. Helmut was a murderer. Nevertheless, he did know he wanted to hear the rest as he watched her lift her face. It was wet from tears.

"Take your time, Harriet," Mr. McMichael warmly comforted. He pushed the box of tissues toward her and leaned back in his chair. Matt watched him, wondering if he knew the entire story or not.

"I didn't do it," Mrs. Helmut began again, a crack in her voice. "Raymond got one of his lawyer friends to represent me in court. The trial lasted a couple of weeks. I was nearly found guilty. At the last minute, Raymond discovered a log entry in Patty's electronic diary. This opened up further investigations that lead to suicide." She wiped her eyes.

"That's not the end of it all, was it?" Mr. McMichael asked.

Incredible! thought Matt. *This guy knows the entire story. Nothing escapes him.* He turned to see if Joey was still in the doorway listening and found the whole group of boys standing as quiet as statues, all of them staring at their foster mother feeling a little poignant.

"No. That wasn't the end. It was the beginning. After the trial, Raymond approached me." She paused in order to form the next sentences in her mind. "He told me he created the computer files that lead to the not guilty verdict. He told me he still believed it was me that killed his wife, my sister."

Everyone gave her a moment to wipe her eyes and blow her nose.

"That's when the extortion started." It was more of a statement than a question.

She nodded yes. "First I sold our father's entire estate to him, and liquidated all my assets. He wanted all my sister's books and research untouched. I was forced to move out immediately. I was broke and homeless and then he told me I would be paying for my sister's death the rest of my life. That's how I came into this," she said, looking around the room. She spotted the boys standing in the doorway.

"I'm sorry, boys. I was forced to have you live like this."

"He gave you this house and told you how to collect the money," Mr. McMichael filled in.

"Yes. He even got my foster license for me. I didn't know anything about foster caring. I was an accountant for Trans World Airlines." It seemed much easier for her to talk now. Twelve years of bottling it all up, and it was coming out like a shaken bottle of soda.

"I believe you didn't have anything to do with your sister's death. I also feel for you, being tormented by Raymond Dunston. We've crossed paths before and you're correct, he's not a decent man." Mr. McMichael looked at his watch. "I have a plane leaving in an hour. I am going to leave Kyle and Paul here with you. We've got a plan for you that I am sure you will enjoy, but I am warning you, you must act quickly."

He turned to Matt. "Matthew Malone, would you like to attend Wesley-Hampton Academy?"

Matt felt his face turn red and his own knees go weak. "Wesley-Hampton Academy? You bet!"

The headmaster rolled his chair toward Matt and extended his hand. "Congratulation!" They shook hands. "Now I must ask you to pack; we have a plane to catch."

Matt turned to leave the room as a stampede of boys circled him. Each one wished him good luck and gave him high fives. However, the thought of what was going to happen to each one of them traversed from one to another. Even Matt wondered what his life was now going to be like.

Matt decided that when he got to the airport he would ask what would happen to Mrs. Helmut and the boys. But for now he needed to gather his things. He turned to Joey and said, "Come on, buddy. Help me get my stuff." Joey wiped his eyes and followed Matt from the room.

It took one rainy day in August for a man to walk into their lives and change each of them. He

Howell, MR.   Wesley-Hampton Academy
gave hope to all of them. Restored life to one of them.
Moreover,   he   offered   adventure   and   challenge
unparallel to one very advantageous boy.

Chapter Four
"This is a once in a lifetime storm."
– Tony Miller, Weather Channel

Molly checked her luggage in and sat down in a hard plastic airport chair. People were on the go all around her. For a few moments, she watched a mother and her two children quietly and personally wish their husband and father a safe trip.

Two army soldiers from the post nearby sat down across from her, facing her. A smirk crossed her face as she contemplated whether she could drop the two to the ground. In tournaments, she had often fought outside her division in the past year. Many times she went up against seventeen and eighteen-year-olds. But a controlled fight under the rules of competition was much different compared to a survival of the fittest match. It would be an interesting fight, she contemplated.

For the next hour, her mind and eyes moved from one interesting thing to the next. The most fascinating of all was the newspaper article she glanced at. She skimmed an article on the front page about the weather in Florida. The article, "Heavy Rains Bring Floods; Disney Closes," appeared engaging enough to spend a couple of minutes on. The thought of rain so hard it would close down Disney World made her shiver. She was glad to be heading to the Boston area.

When the boarding call finally arrived and Molly was buckled in her seat on the plane, she began to think about her busy mom. She already knew she was going to miss her, but the excitement ahead was enough to keep other thoughts at bay.

. . .

Matt and Mr. McMichael rode to the Orlando Airport without talking to each other. It wasn't a silent trip, though. Mr. McMichael made several phone calls; most seemed encrypted and unclear. Two calls came in during the trip. The first one lasted only a couple of seconds with Dunston's name being mentioned. The other was a little longer. It was from someone named Connor and Mr. McMichael seemed quite pleased with his team's work. Matt wondered if Connor was a student or a faculty member.

Matt was given a folder to look through that contained pamphlets and sheets of information pertaining to Wesley-Hampton Academy. He knew he was expected to look it all over, except the events of the last hour kept playing in his mind.

The van they rode in didn't stop at the front of the airport, but rather entered through a guarded gate and drove out away from the main terminal building. It finally stopped at one of three jets parked near a small hanger. Nobody went from the van to the building; instead, Matt followed them to the nearest jet that was idly running. Mr. McMichael and his chair were lowered out of the van quickly and he was wheeled into the aircraft.

They were airborne in a matter of minutes.

"That was quick," Matt commented to Mr. McMichael, but received no response.

Several minutes passed in silence until Mr. McMichael set his papers down and turned toward Matt. "Follow me."

The two made their way to a conference room in the middle of the plane. Matt took a seat.

"I need to apologize to you, Matt. I am quite involved in a situation that seems to be getting worse."

Matt smiled shyly and said nothing.

Straight away, Mr. McMichael answered Matt's question without even being asked. "I have made arrangements for your former foster mother and the other boys. I have given Mrs. Helmut a chance to start over and escape her past. She will be well protected from Raymond." He continued, "As for the boys, they will be placed in a wonderful foster home in Tampa where arrangements will be made to get as many of them adopted as possible. The future looks bright for everyone."

Matt thought of his friend Joey. The prospect of him being adopted and having a family with a mom and a dad brought a tear to his eyes. Would there be a chance of him being adopted too? He didn't mention anything about his own possibility for a future family. Matt's thoughts broke off as Mr. McMichael changed the subject.

"You're a smart young man, Matt. I received your application and was very impressed. The letter and conversations I had with Mr. Clifton were also impressive."

An embarrassed grin returned to Matt's face.

"I need to rush this along. I couldn't stay in the area for long. I hope you didn't mind." Mr. McMichael watched him shake his head and mouth the word "no."

"I'm sure you have a great many questions for me. Before you ask them let me explain Wesley-Hampton Academy," Mr. McMichael began. "It is a school that was started nearly sixty years ago. We search the county looking for students that demonstrate an expertise in certain areas and invite them to attend our campus. We are located just outside Boston, in a secluded location."

He paused and pressed a button on the table. A map lit up on the wall behind him. It displayed the United Stated with a large red dot near the city marked Boston.

"Here we work with each student honing their talents and providing them with new skills and abilities. We look at what the individual has and how we can expand on it. The process of learning we use is state-of-the-art. I think you will be impressed."

Matt felt like he should ask a question or two but couldn't think of anything to ask. Everything sounded like any other school he heard about. At the foster home he was homeschooled, if you could call it that. Most of the time the older boys taught the younger boys reading and math. Matt learned a great deal from reading books.

Mr. McMichael continued, "We use these skills to problem solve. The students work in teams and have assignments that they must complete. I think I will have you sit down with your team when we get to Wesley-Hampton. They can fill you in on all the details. You and another student, Molly, will be joining an established veteran team: Connor, Julie, and Doug. They're a good team, hard workers."

Matt wondered if it was the same Connor from the phone call.

"I have some work to get done. Why don't you just enjoy our flight and look over the information I gave you."

Matt nodded and Mr. McMichael left the room.

. . .

Molly watched out her window as the plane left the ground and she felt her stomach tighten as the adventure began. Once the plane reached cruising altitude, she selected a news show to watch on the little TV screen on the back of the seat in front of her.

Again, the weather in Florida was a big item in the news. She listened to the newscast and watched the video.

"The weather in Florida hasn't changed in the past four days as a bizarre weather system seems to have stalled over the Orlando area. Many people have been evacuated from their homes as this storm has dropped more than eight inches to the area.

"Disney World has shut their gates the last two days, sending tourists to their hotels during their Southeastern vacation. This has undoubtedly cost the Disney Corporation, as well as others, a great deal of tourist dollars.

"Weather forecasters have no solid theory that can explain this weather anomaly, but they all agree it is a once in a lifetime event. As destructive as this system has been, it has been equally fascinating to watch."

Molly continued to watch the news until she dosed off to sleep. The flight attendant woke her as the plane made its final descent into the Boston airport. She was as ready as she'd ever be.

Chapter Five
"Welcome to Wesley-Hampton Academy.
I'm here to help you."
– SYLVIA

Wesley-Hampton Academy was not what Matt had expected. There was no old brick school-like building; instead, the academy was a modern single story building that looked more like an office complex. Rows of windows filled one side of the structure. Above a set of double doors, which slid open as they approached, were the words *Service Entrance— Authorized Personnel Only*. He followed behind Mr. McMichael into the building through the parted doors into a hallway of office doors. Matt passed plaques beside each door and wondered if B. Hunter, J. Overton, K. St. Lucia, L. Richardson, or T. Hampton were teachers. They stopped outside of the room labeled D. McMichael, Headmaster. Matt waited while Mr. McMichael dropped a package off and closed his door.

They walked silently down several hallways and entered through a door after Mr. McMichael pressed his thumb on a light green square on the wall. The hall was carpeted green and a broad green stripe was painted across the center of both walls.

"You are in the Green Wing, Matt."

Each door was painted green and beside the doors were name plaques similar to the ones he saw earlier.   On each one were three names. He counted four sets of names, all girls. They reached the end of the hall and passed through a set of doors that Mr. McMichael opened again with a press of his thumb.

Fingerprint coded, thought Matt.   He wondered how many people had access.

Down this hall, Matt saw the same tri-named doors as before, only this time they were boy names.

They stopped at one room entrance and Matt noticed the small light green pad for the first time next to door handle. Mr. Michael pressed his thumb and said, "Recognize and record Matthew Malone." He removed his thumb and the square turned red. "Matt, the system needs to record your thumb print. We use it for security. All you need to do is press your thumb on the pad and then pull it away."

Mr. Michael rolled away from the door and allowed Matt to approach the pad. Matt fisted his left hand and extended his thumb. He pressed the pad. It turned blue and returned to green after the moment he removed his thumb.

"*Welcome to Wesley-Hampton Academy, Matthew Malone,*" said a woman's voice, tranquil with a touch of a British accent. Matt tried to figure out where the voice was coming from but couldn't. It seemed to be echoing from all around.

Mr. McMichael laughed for a moment. "That's SYLVIA. She's our computer. She's waiting for a thank you."

Matt felt rather ridiculous talking to an invisible person and thought he might be part of a prank. Hesitantly he responded, "Thank you."

"*You're more than welcome.*" The voice was authentic. It didn't have a tinny or metallic sound. It sounded rather motherly, as if it cared. "*You're now in the system, Matthew Malone. Would it be okay if I called you Matt?*"

"Sure," he responded, looking, for lack of anywhere else, at the green square.

"Would you like to go in the room now?" Mr. McMichael gestured toward the door. "Go on in. Your roommates won't be here until tomorrow. They're in Italy right now."

Italy, Matt repeated in his head. He wondered if it was common to travel outside the United States. He wondered if he would get the chance to see other parts of the world. What a difference from his foster home! The thought made him smile.

"It will give you time to freshen up before dinner."

"Yeah, I guess so," Matt said hesitantly.

The door to the room opened. *"Let me know if I can help you in any way,"* the maternal British voice offered.

"I will see you at dinner," the headmaster said as he headed away down the hall.

Matt broke his gaze from the room and looked at the departing wheelchair. "Where do I go for dinner?"

"If you have any questions about anything, feel free to ask SYLVIA," the man instructed and he was gone.

Matt stood alone in the hallway thinking about where he was a few hours ago and the friends he left behind. He wondered if they had moved out of 421 Sycamore yet. It was hard to think of Mrs. Helmut as a victim, but the story that played out was fascinating and mysterious all in one.

He walked in the room and the door silently closed behind him.

Matt was stunned by the appearance within. There were the basic things anyone would expect to find: three beds, desks, and closets. However, it was the extra things that astonished him. On the left wall was a huge screen. Matt assumed the eight-foot wide, five-foot high panel was plasma. He had never seen one so large. In front was a table with a keyboard and mouse.   Three chairs surrounded the table.   A computer? he wondered.   On the opposite wall was another panel, but only half the size. This one was on and active.   It displayed names and groups. Each group was colored: red, green, blue, orange, black, and turquoise. Matt noticed several of the names he had seen earlier at the doors displayed in full color.

He scanned the names. *Matt M.* was written in dark green and next to it were the words *In Room 13.* Below his name was the name *Molly O. Just arriving.* Above his name were three others: *Julie J., Italy; Connor O., Italy; Doug W., Italy.* There were three other groups of names in green. It was the largest collection of names. The other colors had one or two teams, but each team had as many as eight names. At the bottom was a legend. Matt read it:

Orange–Research
Red–Finance
Black–Assignment Managing
Turquoise–Technology/SYLVIA
Blue–Educational Management
Green–Field

"Field," he said aloud. "What does field mean?"

"Did you need some help, Matt?" the English speaking voice asked.

Matt spun around, startled. "What?"

"Did you want to know what 'field' meant?"

"Can you tell me?"

"Field is what you are assigned to."

Matt tilted his head. "Do you think you could be more descriptive? What kind of school is this?"

"Of course I can be. I'll answer your last question, since the answer to that might clear up other things you're wondering."

Matt was about to say something when the plasma screen in front of him lit up. A view of Wesley-Hampton Academy appeared from an angle he hadn't seen. It showed a parking lot in front of the school and large front doors under a sign that read: *Welcome to Wesley-Hampton Academy.* The image froze for a few seconds and then began to rotate downward, revealing an aerial view. When the image stopped turning, the roof vanished and displayed the layout of the rooms below. The image then switched to portraits of two men.

"Wesley-Hampton Academy was founded in 1941 by William Wesley and Benjamin Hampton. It was first designed to help break the German codes during World War II. William and Benjamin used

students from the local high school and successfully broke the entire code and was instrumental in bringing an end to the war in Europe."

Matt sat down in one of the chairs at the table.

"During the war years the school received funding from the government for its efforts. Both Wesley and Hampton were close personal friends of then President Franklin D. Roosevelt and were part of the government's intelligence gathering community. Before President Roosevelt's death, he established a funding and a purpose for the school. To this day that funding and purpose still exists."

"What is the purpose?"

"The purpose of this school is to provide state-of-the-art education to a small number of students. The government provides the funding to create new technologies for the purpose of education. These technologies are put into practice and evaluated for future use in tomorrow's public schools. In exchange, the school monitors and intervenes in matters of national security."

"Wait a minute!" Matt yelled out. "In exchange the school monitors and intervenes in matters of national security? I'm being trained to be a spy?"

"Well not exactly, Matt. You are being trained to help prevent a breakdown in our national security."

"How is that not spying?"

"You will not be directly doing any detective or espionage work. You will be asked to assist other team members and other teams in schemes to stop plots already in motion. Your job is very critical."

"Let me get this straight. I work with other students to stop terrorists from planning and executing terrorist acts on our country."

"Yes."

"And get killed!"

"No."

"You mean in sixty years no one has ever gotten killed?"

"That would be correct. Although we have had two accidental deaths in the school during those sixty years, none have been during field time. They were during practice sessions."

Matt struggled for something to say. His mind reeled in several different directions.

"Would you like to see a list of people who have gone to Wesley-Hampton Academy that you might recognize?"

With this question now posed, Matt's brain stopped all thinking and he responded affirmatively.

Howell, MR.   Wesley-Hampton Academy

The screen displayed a list of names in two columns. Matt scanned the list. He recognized only a few of the names. Most notably were two senators' names that he remembered hearing about in the news and another name was a former president of the United States. Matt was very impressed. As he stared at the list, he began to wonder how his name would look someday.

"*Matt.*"

Matt shook his head clear. "Yeah."

"*It's nearly time for dinner.*"

It took Matt a moment to switch gears and start thinking about food. "What time is dinner, SYLVIA?"

"*5:00 p.m. Do you need a map?*"

"No, I think I can find it. Thanks for the information, SYLVIA."

As his mind raced a hundred miles an hour, the realization hit him hard. He was part of something much bigger than he ever imagined, and he hoped he could handle the challenge.

Chapter Six
"SYLVIA, who is Raymond Dunston?"
– Molly

Molly watched Matt enter the room looking confused. She recognized that same feeling when she arrived only a few minutes earlier. She watched him as he took in everything in the room. He noticed the tables immediately. They were white with a colored band around each one. Matt recognized the colors from the chart on his room's wall. They all were represented and occupied by other students. Each group of tables was full except the green table, which had only four students. He also noticed one long table at the front of the room with adults seated at it. In the middle was Mr. McMichael, flanked by four people on each side. Teachers, he reasoned.

Not wanting to draw too much attention to himself, he headed toward the tables trimmed in green. A red-haired girl smiled at him as he approached.

"Hi. You must be Matthew Malone."

Matt sat down in the chair next to hers and returned a nervous smile. He nodded and scanned the faces of the other students in the room. Most were eating. Many of them held conversations with someone near while a few were busy reading or writing.

"My name's Molly. I just got here."

"Hi, my name's Matt. You already knew that."

She smiled, again. Her brown eyes blended smoothly with her hair color and accented her freckle-filled face. "I saw your name on the locator board in my room. SYLVIA told me you were from Florida. I'm from Seattle."

Matt watched Molly pick up a carrot and bite it and realized he hadn't eaten in several hours. "Where did you get the food?" he asked.

Molly explained the cafeteria-style serving and he left in pursuit of a tray. When Matt finally returned to the table, Molly noticed his choices. His plate held three pieces of chicken, mashed potatoes, two rolls, a pile of green beans, and a pear. It was completely covered.

"They didn't feed you in Florida or something?"

"It's a long story. I'm not sure you would believe it."

"Try me," Molly said.

Matt told her about the house and Mrs. Helmut. He told her about the meals and jobs. Finally, he told her about Mr. McMichael.

Molly listened while she ate until Matt mentioned Mr. McMichael. She looked up at the front table and back at Matt. "You rode in *his* jet. Wow!"

It didn't seem to be a big deal to Matt and he couldn't understand Molly's reaction.

Molly was impressed with Matt's tale, including the Raymond Dunston part. It seemed significant, but she couldn't figure out how. They both agreed to ask SYLVIA when dinner was finished.

For the remainder of the meal the two talked about their hometowns. At the conclusion of mealtime, Mr. McMichael addressed the students present. He made some comments to the Research team and arranged a meeting with the Assignment-Management team. The last thing he states was he wanted the new school members to stay behind for a few minutes. Everyone else was dismissed.

Matt and Molly cleaned up their trays and gathered near the front table with six other students.

"I would like to welcome you all to Wesley-Hampton Academy. My name is Mr. McMichael. We are very happy to have you here. We hope you have found everything comfortable. If you have questions,

SYLVIA is always nearby. I would like to introduce you to our staff."

Mr. McMichael wheeled around the table to the front where the eight students stood in a bunch. He stopped at the first person seated at the end of the table. "This is Ms. Richardson, and she works with the red team: Finance. She's also your math instructor."

The students examined the smiling teacher who said nothing. She quietly stood, nodded, and sat back down. Mr. McMichael moved onto the next person.

"This is Mr. Hunter. He will be working with orange team, which is Research. Mr. Hunter will be your library assistant and homework helper."

The black, curly-haired man stood. His standing height was not much taller than when sitting. At only five-one, he was the shortest staff member. "I am also the one you will want to see before turning in any term papers. I am quite sure none of you can construct a decent essay." He sat down.

Mr. McMichael continued down the table. In contrast to Mr. Hunter, Mr. Hampton stood at six foot ten inches tall. He was by far the tallest staff member and the tallest person any of the eight students had ever met. Matt and the others were amazed how large he was. His arms were as thick as tree limbs and he appeared to have no neck.

"This is Mr. Hampton; he is the advisor to the blue team, which is Educational Management."

"I over see your education here at W-H. If you need to know how you are doing you will need to make an appointment to see me," the giant of a man told them. "I am also your physical education instructor."

"Mr. Hampton is also the temporary advisor for the black team, the Assignment/Management team. We are looking to fill that vacancy," Mr. McMichael told them as Mr. Hampton sat down. "I don't think Arnold Schwarzenegger would like to run into him in a dark alley." The students laughed.

"Next is our groundskeeper, Mr. Overton."

A white-haired man with a scruffy white beard and white unkempt eyebrows stood halfway up and then sat back down. Matt remembered seeing the names of each person next to an office door earlier. He wondered why a groundskeeper needed an office with the rest of the staff.

Mr. McMichael introduced the school's secretary, Ms. Wendell, and moved to the last person. Before he had a chance to say anything, the fair-haired man on the end stood up.

"What a fine crop of students, Mr. McMichael," he said in a deep English accent. "I am

Mr. St. Lucia. I am the Technology team director and I will be your science teacher."

"Mr. St. Lucia was the creator of SYLVIA, our school's computer."

"Well, you know. We Brits have an edge on you Americans when it comes to computers. What can I say?"

"Thank you, Mr. St. Lucia. And if you were wondering, I am the director of the Field team," Mr. McMichael said, rolling back toward the students. "Staff, I would like you to meet our new students. Brian and Lucy are our new Research team members. Terry and Marquise are our new Tech. team members. Matt, Molly, and Johanna are new Field team members, and Wendy is our new Finance member." The staff offered a warm applause.

Mr. McMichael turned back to the students. "On your beds you will all find the uniform for classes and a schedule. Classes begin tomorrow so I recommend plenty of sleep. As I said earlier, if you have any questions tonight, don't hastate to ask SYLVIA. Do any of you have any questions for us?"

After answering several logistic questions, the students were dismissed to their dorm rooms. Molly told Matt she had seen computers in the library she passed on her way to dinner. He followed as she led them in that direction. They had decided halfway to the library to ask who Raymond Dunston was and what his connection was to Wesley-Hampton Academy. They also wanted to know where to go to get to their classes in the morning.

The library was an enormous room lined with shelves of books. In the center were dozens of tables, most arranged in groups. On the far wall were blank computer screens, similar to the one in Matt's room. The two sat down in front of a computer screen. Looking up at the blank screen, Matt felt excited and curious. What if they were delving into something that was way over their heads? He wondered if there were restrictions to the information in the data banks.

Molly wondered the same thing, but chose to send caution to the proverbial wind and asked, "SYLVIA, who is Raymond Dunston?"

SYLVIA came to life.

Chapter Seven
"Headmaster!" – Molly

A picture of a man with a dark, well-trimmed beard appeared on the screen. Below the picture the caption read:

Raymond E. Dunston, Headmaster 1985–1995.

"Headmaster," Molly said. "SYLVIA, why did he leave Wesley-Hampton Academy?"

"Mr. Dunston requested a leave of absence on December 7th, 1995."

"Why?" Matt asked.

"Most of the information dealing with Mr. Dunston is unavailable at this time."

"What can you tell us?" Molly asked.

"SYLVIA, cancel that request." Molly and Matt turned around and looked at the source of the last command. Mr. St. Lucia stood directly behind them. "It would not be a good idea to continue your present inquiries. Raymond Dunston is not your concern."

Molly's face competed with her hair for the brightest red color and her cheeks were winning. "We didn't know he was off limits. We were just curious."

"I understand. You would not be the first students to venture into areas you're not allowed. I would suggest the two of you return to your dorms. You have a busy day tomorrow, with me." Mr. St. Lucia smiled and backed up a step to allow them to pass.

As they walked away, they heard the technology teacher tell SYLVIA to deep-freeze any information pertaining to Raymond Edward Dunston and RED Technologies.

"I wonder what all that was about, Matt. It sounds like Dunston will just have to remain an enigma."

"I hope we didn't get into any trouble. That's all we need on our first day." They both laughed nervously.

Matt reached his room and pressed the green pad and entered. Everything was the way he left it, except the five identical shirts on the end of his bed. He held one up. It was a dark green pullover and had the words "Wesley-Hampton" in an arch on the upper left side in yellow. Under the school's name was Team 2.

Next to the pile of shirts was a gadget like the one he had seen at the foster home earlier in the day. Matt picked it up. It was the size of a paperback book and no thicker than half an inch. On the front was a rectangular screen that was bordered with rows of buttons; three buttons on the left and right going vertical and eight split horizontally across the top and bottom. When Matt's finger touched the screen, it lit up, startling him. On the screen, Matt saw his name and under it the words *SYLVIA's Personal Assistant* appeared. Along the sides, corresponding to the columns of buttons, were choices. On the left were *Ask SYLVIA*, *Calendar*, and *International Dictionary*. On the opposite side were *Schedule*, *E-mail*, and *Internet*.

Matt pressed the *Schedule* button and watched his class schedule appear.

He looked his schedule over for a few minutes, making a mental note of his first class in the morning: 7:30 a.m. Computer Lab.

After checking with SYLVIA on the location of the lab, he decided to get some sleep. It was the first time in his life he had ever slept alone. Oddly enough, it didn't feel very comfortable.

Chapter Eight
"That's a blizzard!"
– Marquise Fuller

The first half of day one of classes went rather slow for both Matt and Molly. They sat the morning away answering questions in individual booths. SYLVIA tested each of the new students at terminals in compartments. The compartments were part of the vast computer lab at Wesley-Hampton Academy. As Mr. St. Lucia put it, "SYLVIA is the brain of this school, no matter what Mr. McMichael says."

The questions that each were asked ranged from mathematics to science to government. They were to allow SYLVIA to map out a plan of study for each student and create a three dimensional image of each student's knowledge. The image would show the depth and intensity the student possessed in the overall curriculum, and the information would show areas of interest a student might have for extended lessons.

By lunchtime, neither Molly nor Matt's roommates had returned. Matt did notice when he stopped at his room that the locator panel showed them as in transit back to the school.

During the second half of the day things improved, and Mr. St. Lucia treated the students to a trip to SYLVIA's room. Molly had never seen such a computer before. Hidden within a room the size of a small house were rows of gray and black cabinets. Digital readouts displaying the temperature and computing speed appeared at intervals along the row of cabinets, and in large red block letters the word SYLVIA was labeled on all sides.

Matt stood in amazement. His eyes, like saucers, scanned the entire room from the row of thirty cabinets to the four enormous plasma screens that appeared on one entire wall. He slowly began to move around the room reading one panel and then the next.

Mr. St. Lucia caught up to him as he neared the far wall. The partition was entirely made of a clear polymer. It was like a giant plastic window, but it was the other side of the synthetic glass that grabbed Matt's attention.

"Is there a question you have about anything?"

Matt stared at a Jell-O-like substance as thousands of blue sparks flashed before him like fireworks seen from above. "Is that a Lucid

Crystallized Diffusion?" he asked with his eyes glued to the scene.

"I beg your pardon, Matt," Mr. St. Lucia exclaimed. "How do you know about this?"

Still staring he said, "I've read about it in magazines. I thought it was only a theory. No one has ever been able to keep one together for more then a few nanoseconds."

"Well, actually it is a form of the LCD theory, only I made several small modifications to it. For example, instead of using liquid oxygen . . ." he began.

"You used liquid hydrogen," Matt cut him off, taking the breath right out of Mr. St Lucia's chest and ego. "That would explain the blue color to the static discharge."

"Are you sure you're assigned correctly, Mr. Malone? How did Mr. McMichael get you in fieldwork? He's up to something again. I can feel it."

Matt ignored the computer teacher's comments. "Is that entire LCD tank SYLVIA's only memory core?"

Still impressed with the young boy's knowledge, Mr. St. Lucia slowly answered, "We have three others. One acts as the central core and one we use as a compressed backup. The third is SYLVIA's 'long-term' memory and this one acts more like a 'short term' memory.   None very full, she's got room to grow."

Matt purposefully turned from the memory jell and looked back at the large cabinets. "An Intel 512 Itanium 3 processor and, if I'm not mistaken, that's a combination of the British computer SGI Altix 3800 called the Newton and CRAY's T3E1800/ 1084 super computer."

"I'm completely astounded with your knowledge, Matt. How do you know so much about computer processors?"

"Well, let's just say I had plenty of time to read before coming here.   May I ask a couple questions?"

"Sure."

"How did you get the two companies to combine Newton and CRAY to create this?"

"It wasn't easy. It was arranged with the help of a couple multibillion-dollar grants for each company. It is the only computer like it in the entire world. The plans for SYLVIA were destroyed as she was being built. The only glitch was the sudden death of one of its creators. She was instrumental in the construction of this computer. Other than that, it was a foolproof project, completely unduplicatable."

Matt looked at the plasma screens on the wall and watched the numbers, letters, and symbols move rapidly across the screen. "I've never actually used it before, but it looks like UNIX, am I right?"

"Yes you are, Matt. Actually, it is a special form of UNIX developed by some colleagues of mine back in York, England. They call it Yorky-Unix. Pretty original, don't you think?" Mr. St. Lucia's eyes caught the last panel as an image of the United States appeared and then the state of Minnesota lit up and expanded to the full size of the screen. An area near Minneapolis was framed and it took over as the main image. A pink and white mass was seen to move toward a region near the city. The mass disappeared and then reformed and moved toward the same spot again. This cycle continued.

Mr. St. Lucia went from light-hearted to gravely serious in one short-lived moment. "I think we'll have to discontinue this tour," he told the students. "SYLVIA, send the map image immediately to all staff members and continue to monitor for any changes."

He escorted the students to the lab's door and instructed them to head back to their rooms and prepare for dinner. The students watched him depart and without delay head for one of SYLVIA's terminals.

Once in the hallway the students began chattering about the abrupt termination to the tour.

"Did you see the map image on the screen?" Molly asked. "It looked like one I saw on the airplane yesterday. The only difference was the color. The one I saw was green and blue."

"I know what that was," Marquise said. "I'm from northern North Dakota. That's a blizzard heading toward Minneapolis. I've seen a lot of those on the Weather Channel. I've just never seen one come out of nowhere before."

They all looked at the dark-haired, dark-skinned boy and wondered what was so important about a blizzard thousands of miles away.

.   .   .

By evening, Matt's roommates had returned. They greeted each other and exchanged information about hometowns, favorites, and past adventures. Matt was intrigued by the stories Connor shared. He had been at the academy longer than Doug and had completed many more assignments.

Connor told of assignments in London, Tokyo, Sydney, and various places throughout the United States. None of the tasks sounded completely dangerous; in fact, they sounded fun. Matt liked the story of when Connor and some other students met the Queen of England.

Matt told them about his former foster home and how Mr. McMichael came all the way to Florida to pick him up. Doug and Connor were equally impressed by Matt's story.

The three talked until it was nearly 11:00 p.m. They would have kept the conversation alive longer had SYLVIA not reminded them of the time.

Breakfast the next morning was much livelier then the previous meals now that the entire Green Team was back. Mr. McMichael opened the day with a few remarks about keeping the noise down between classes and something about a lost "SPA." Connor read the confused look on Matt's face and explained that it meant "SYLVIA's Personal Assistant."

"Don't ever lose yours," Doug advised him from across the table. "Julie lost one in Baton Rouge one time."

"What happened?" Molly asked.

"I had to write an essay about the reasons I need my SPA and how I should treat it. Eight pages," Julie added with a sigh.

Mr. McMichael continued. "I would like to thank all the members of the Green Team for a job well done. I understand there was a nicely performed bike crash I missed. I might need to ask for a reenactment."

The room broke into laughter. "I don't think so!" Julie told the students around her.

"And one last thing—I will need to see the Research Team immediately following breakfast."

"I wonder if that has to do with the storm we saw on the screen yesterday?" Molly said.

Curiosity spread from person to person in the small nook of friends. Doug asked about the storm image and Molly and Matt explained what they saw and what happened in the computer room. They also told everyone about Marquise's assumption.

"I would say it must be what the buzz is all about," Julie concluded.

"Well, it looks like we don't have much of a break between assignments this time," Connor told them.

Doug smiled. "It beats the classwork any day."

Chapter Nine
"Research is the backbone to every mission."
– Mr. Hunter

Matt and Molly were to report to the computer lab at the end of breakfast for the second day in a row: more testing. By lunchtime, the two hoped there would be no more testing. They met Doug, Connor, and Julie at the green tables and were told there were some things that happened while they were testing. Mr. McMichael called together a meeting with the entire Green Team at 1:30 this afternoon.

None of them knew what the meeting was about, but Conner told them that a friend of his in research mentioned something interesting.

"Beth fessed up about something that her team was working on. She said they have intensely searched for information on Raymond Dunston."

Matt and Molly exchanged a knowing glance. "That's a name I've heard a lot of in the past two days," Matt told them. "He was headmaster here about ten years ago."

"We were looking him up when Mr. St. Lucia told the computer to stop. He told it to put the information in deep freeze or something," Molly added.

"Well, we'll all find out at 1:30," Doug injected.

They all finished lunch and headed for the briefing room. It was large lecture hall with more plasma screens adorning the walls, these being as large as those in SYLVIA's room. One of the screens showed a map of the United States. Matt noticed a red circle marked the area near his former foster home. There were four other circles in different places on the map.

Matt followed the others to a row of seats. Each seat slid forward to a table that had a computer keyboard and screen built into it. He watched the other students press the green button on the table near their computer. It was the same fingerprint security pad that was outside his room. He pressed his and the pad went blue. Immediately his computer screen, which was tilted below the surface of the table for easy visibility, changed to a "WELCOME MATT" screen. It then took on the same image that was displayed on the giant screen.

Molly nudged Matt in the side. "Here comes Mr. McMichael."

Matt looked down the inclined rows and saw the headmaster rolling his wheelchair up to a table at the front. He met with Mr. St. Lucia, Ms. Wendell, and Mr. Hunter for a couple of minutes and then the cluster split up. The three teachers left Mr. McMichael and found seats in the front row as he switched on a microphone and addressed the students.

"Thank you for getting here on time. I don't want to delay any longer than we have to. It looks like we have a situation that is growing out of control." The circles on the map of the United States began to flash. "There is a person out there, as we speak, that is raging havoc on the populations of our cities."

Mr. McMichael paused to allow everyone to grasp the severity of the situation. He rolled from the table and lit a laser pointer. The red dot moved across the screen and landed on the red circle in Florida. "We had a major rain storm near Miami that has all but paralyzed the city."

He moved the pointer to the ring around San Francisco. "Next, a fog settled into the city by the bay. Not their typical fog; this one is thick and has lasted for four days now. All transportation, both air and ground, have been halted."

The red pointer shifted to southern California to the mark around San Diego. "The temperatures in the San Diego area have dropped to 5 degrees above zero for the past three days. The zoo and other tourist places have shut down. There are freezing water pipes all over the region." The pointer moved to Minnesota. "Another cold location is Minneapolis. Although the residents there are accustomed to the cold, they were not completely prepared for the blizzard that hit yesterday. The storm, like all the rest of the natural disasters, has settled into the locale and is moving very slowly. As of one hour ago, it has been reported that 37 inches of snow have fallen. With the biting cold and 30 mile per hour winds, the St. Paul/Minneapolis region is completely shut down. Oddly enough, the deepest snowfall occurred around the Mall of America.

"And just this morning a series of hail storms have been popping up over Nebraska, Iowa, and Illinois. Entire fields of crops have been wiped out," he told them as his pointer touched the large circle encompassing the three states.

The red laser beam disappeared and Mr. McMichael rolled back to the table. "I would like to turn this over to Mr. Hunter now."

The short man stood up and turned to the students. He tugged on the back of his sport coat and adjusted the knot in his necktie. "My research team has been at work for many hours this morning," he began. "We looked at each of the weather anomalies and have made a few unconfirmed conclusions."

The big screen on the opposite wall came to life. The deductions made by the investigating team appeared:

1.   Each storm displayed a different weather phenomenon.

2.   Four out of five targeted largely populated regions.

3.   Each storm crippled economic fronts.

4.   The storms do not move like normal storms.

5.   They disappear as abruptly as they appeared.

Mr. Hunter explained each of the points. "We then went to SYLVIA. We asked her if these storms could be manmade. She concluded the technology is not there yet, but the pattern indicates human intervention. He paused for a moment as the screen changed to a map of the United States. It was similar to the map on the opposite wall, except it was void of the circles and displayed light blue lines crisscrossing in every direction. Each heavily inhabited area was a converging of lines so dense they created large blue masses.

"We asked SYLVIA what would be needed to create such storms and one of the components she deduced was electricity. So we asked her to monitor the electrical output on the nation's power grid. That's when we hit pay dirt!" Mr. Hunter's voice grew excited. "SYLVIA monitored the grid throughout the morning and one hour ago we watched a surprising occurrence."

Mr. Hunter turned away from the class, more for effect then practicality. "SYLVIA, play the grid file from this morning and annotate, please."

"Yes, Mr. Hunter," SYLVIA agreed. *"On the map is the energy output for the entire continental United States. At exactly 9:33 a.m. EST the grid was functioning normally, but at 9:34 it changed. The change was for only about 3.5 seconds and looked like this."*

Everyone was glued to the map on the wall or his or her computer screen and listening to SYLVIA's narration. The blue lines pulsed on the screen. As the clock in the corner changed from 9:33 to 9:34, something strange happened in northern Texas. The blue around the Dallas, Fort Worth, and Plaino area all began to fade to white and a small spot to the north lit up. The tiny region went from nothing to a glowing dark blue speck on a line running toward the three cities.

All eyes turn back toward Mr. Hunter. "As you can see, the power grid shows a drain of power in the Dallas area and surge of power to a location north of the region.   This rush of power occurred as the storms were breaking over the Midwest fields. As SYLVIA pointed out, the surge lasted only 3.5 seconds and did not cause any disruptions to the metropolitan expanse. When we looked back over the last five days, we recorded four more power spikes. Each coincided with a different weather episode."

The map on the wall changed, again.   An expanded area of northern Texas replaced the previous picture.   The blue lines were gone.   A small arrow overlaid on the map pointed to a bleak area.

"As we narrowed down the location, we asked SYLVIA to provide us with the latest satellite image of the site."   The map began to change as the image increased magnification.

Matt watched on his computer screen as roads and farmhouses appeared.   The resolution was incredible.   He could see cars and a truck on the road. Trees and fences could be seen clearly, but it was the structure in the middle of a desolate field that stood out the most.   It was completely out of place.   It was white and modern with rounded towers on the north and south sides.   The structure was two stories tall and half the size of a football field.   No roads led to the building; it was entirely cut off and alone.

"Thank you, Mr. Hunter.   Your team did an excellent job," Mr. McMichael confirmed, rolling back to the limelight. Mr. Hunter thanked him and returned to his seat. "That building you are looking at is the source of the storms. We know that with 100% certainly. We also know that we were meant to find it." He closed his blue eyes for a moment as if he was very tired. When he reopened them, he continued. The image on the screens throughout the lecture hall zoomed in further.

"We found something that we feel was predestined for us to find."

Chapter Ten
"The only thing more fun than a stick of dynamite is a truck load of C-2. Always think big!"
– Raymond Dunston

The image, amazingly, continued to magnify. Molly and the rest of the Green Team watched as the building grew larger and larger. The foliage around the structure moved off the edges of the screen as the building itself took up the entire screen. The zooming continued as a small speck on the roof of the edifice grew bigger. As it came more into focus, it was evidently a piece of paper. The duct tape could be seen holding it in place, as well as the writing.

Matt was stunned at the clarity of the satellite image. It was as if the paper was photographed ten feet away, not thousands of miles away. He looked at Connor, who was looking at the picture as if it was commonplace. The enlarging stopped. It was a letter. Matt read it silently.

My dearest friend, McMichael,

I am very disappointed in the length of time it has taken you to find me. Not that an earlier discovery could possibly have stopped any of the events from occurring.

You might be curious as to where all this fun is leading. Well, it is quite simple. Over the past ten years I have been gathering information and technologies that, when combined, have allowed me to affect the atmosphere. I can, in fact, create any type of weather system I wish, but you've already figured that out. Thanks no less to that oversized calculator. Sorry, Lucia.

Ultimately, I plan to bring the nation's tourist and agricultural industries to their knees. As they are finding out at this moment the weather is not something they can count on, but I am. I am arranging to provide all those who have the funds a perfect climate. For a nominal fee, I will grant them the weather of their choice. Just think: no more droughts on the plains, no more vacations ruined by rain. In addition, for those who can't or won't pay, we'll see how long they survive.

Now, I imagine you are asking yourself how I fit into all this. It's simple. As you have probably already deduced, this building is not the one you want. This is just a power transfer site. From here, the electricity collected leaves the nation's grid. From here, it powers my main building. If you or the government destroy this site, I will bring another on line. The public might accept one misguided missile or obliteration of a civilian building, but how many after that? I can keep turning on other sites, but I'm sure there are not enough excuses to go around. You and your school of brats are the only thing standing in my way. I know you have the technology to find me and possibly even destroy me, but I have safeguards in place. I have a weather system more devastating than any other and I have it aimed on your beloved school. It is programmed into my computer and is password-activated. If I don't put in the password when prompted at least once a day, the computer will create the anomaly. Then it's GOOD-BYE Wesley-Hampton.

But understand, I don't want to annihilate your school, so I beg you to stay away. The fate of the students and school rests in your hands, McMichael. Make the right decision.

Sincerely,
Dunston

Silence permeated the room. No one spoke. As each student read the letter, his or her focus turned to the man in the wheelchair. When it appeared that everyone had read it at least once, the solitary figure spoke.

"As you might have guessed, Mr. Dunston and I go way back. In fact, he was the headmaster here prior to my appointment. He was instrumental in the early phases of SYLVIA's construction and I have no doubt he knows our capabilities. He wants us to sit back and allow him to extort money from innocent corporations across this nation. I know Raymond Dunston better than that. This is the start of a major plan. He's not interested in farmer and tourist money. He's only interested in power and big money. I believe he's got his sights set on something much bigger than all this." The classroom of students watched him gently stroke his beard, and from the fourteenth row Matt and the others waited for the next decree.

Without trepidation, he smiled and said, "If we are the only ones capable of stopping him, then I say we stop him!"

A buzz swarmed through the room as the students excitedly plotted with one another. Matt and Molly felt the surge of energy fill the room. It swept through them and coursed in their veins. The thrill both of them yearned for finally arrived. They joined the others in talk of adventure; all the while Dunston's threat loomed in the shadows of the room and minds of the students and staff.

Chapter Eleven
"I would take being in the field over being behind a desk any day."
– Beth Cloven

The rest of the day was filled with restlessness as students and staff moved about the school preparing for the morning. Back at their room, Connor and Doug told Matt about the training and prep that would initiate the next day. The evening belonged to Mr. Hampton and his team. They would work with the Research Team and plan the assignments. Based on the information uncovered, a plan of attack would be developed.

"What happens to classwork?" Matt asked earnestly.

"Everything is put on hold for right now," Doug told him. "Have you been to a learning session yet?"

Matt shook his head.

"Well, they're pretty laid back," Doug said with a laugh. "Literally."

Matt confessed that he wasn't sure what he meant so Doug elaborated. "When you went to the computer lab for testing, you must have seen the cubicles in the back half."

Matt nodded. He remembered seeing the computer on the table in each space and a reclining chair.

"All that testing you did helps SYLVIA determine what you know and what you don't know. She then determines a schedule for your learning."

"What's the chair for?"

"Sleeping," Connor threw in.

Doug laughed. "Actually it is. Once you log in you just sit back and relax. After a few minutes you begin to drift off."

"St. Lucia calls it a trans-like state," Connor explained. "I call it sleep."

"While you're *under*, SYLVIA teaches you things," Doug continued. "It's really cool. When you go to class and start working math problems, everything just starts working for you. It's all up here," he said, tapping his index finger against his head.

"Sounds like brainwashing."

"Not really. Brainwashing is more like erasing what you already know and replacing it with something new. This is just adding onto things you already know," Doug clarified.

"The fun part is your electives. You can pick from a long list of things you want to learn extra," Connor added. "For example, SYLVIA figured out during the testing that I knew a few foreign languages and adapted the sessions to expand my vocabulary and cultural understanding. I picked learning Japanese and reading classics."

"How do you read classics?"

"Actually, SYLVIA reads them to me. It's completely awesome to wake up and know a novel that you didn't know a few hours earlier."

"That's not all you get to do for electives. Some of us stay awake. I'm into karate and swimming," Doug pointed out. "In two years I'm already a blue belt and the fastest swimmer in the school."

"You know," Connor said, pulling up Dunston's letter on the wall monitor, "I bet we get a super assignment this time."

"I wouldn't bet on it, Connor."

"Doug, we can't keep getting set-up assignments."

Matt got up from his chair and walked toward the plasma screen, ignoring his two roommates. He read the entire letter over a couple of times. He was completely absorbed in the letter and didn't hear the knock on the door.

Connor opened the door.

"Got a minute," Beth Cloven asked with a smile. Beth was Connor's closest friend and, unknown to him, his sister's insider. Beth was a tall girl, as tall as Connor. She had straight dark hair, which she always kept cut above her shoulders.

Connor let her in and she handed him a folder. "Hi, Dougie. Julie says hi."

"Hi, Beth," Doug returned with a smile.

"You know what I don't understand?" Matt said, turning around and seeing Beth for the first time.

"Oh. Beth, this is our new teammate and roommate, Matt. Matt, this is Beth. She's on the Research Team."

"Not anymore, Connor. Don't you keep up with the assignment board?"

"Are assignments out already?" Connor asked, moving toward the screen on the wall.

Beth's name was added to Team Two's list. Next to each team member's name was *"prep for investigation."*

"Hey, Beth, you and me on the same team? Nothing will ever be the same again," Doug teased, putting his arm around her waist.

Connor slapped his hips. "That's it!" he yelled out. "We're not even part of the set-up. We're investigation!"

"That's why I came down here," Beth said in a calming voice. "Mr. Hunter assigned me to your team because he needs more information about the building we saw in the satellite image. We found some tire tracks in the weeds heading to the north. We think someone has been there recently." She opened the folder and pulled out a picture of weeds. It wasn't completely clear where the tire marks were until Beth pointed them out.

Matt looked at the picture. As hard as he might, he couldn't see any tire tracks, even after Beth pointed them out to him a second time.

"Look, Connor. This is important. The entire project can't move forward until we check out this site. No one is assigned to anything except us right now."

Connor stared at the screen again. She was correct; none of the other Green Teams had assignments yet. "Well, I guess that's a good sign. Mr. McMichael is at least giving us something to do."

"Hey, it beats sitting around here waiting for another team to finish the investigation," Doug pitched in. "Besides, maybe it will give us an edge in the big mission. What else you got in that folder of yours?"

Beth opened up the folder again and began pulling out papers. She showed the maps of the area and SYLVIA's best speculation of the floor plan. They talked about the new information for the next hour and decided to head down to the cafeteria for supper.

Beth's orange Research Team shirt stood out in the sea of green at the cafeteria table. Everyone was excited to have Beth on the team. Julie had always wanted to have her roommate join her in the field in the past. She always came back and Beth would flood her with questions about the mission. Many times Julie would have an inside tip or two from her discussions with her roomy before the missions.

Beth smiled across the table at Molly. "Are you ready for your first mission?"

"You bet I am. When do we leave?"

"We meet with Mr. Hampton after we finish eating," Connor answered for Beth. "And remember, Molly, I'm team captain. Just because I'm your brother doesn't mean you can do what you want."

"Yes, sir," she responded with a salute.

They laughed and continued eating.

. . .

After eating, the six students of Team Two headed to the gymnasium. Mr. Hampton had a second office off the gym where he spent most of his time. As they entered the massive room, the sound of heavy weights hitting against other weights greeted them. A weight room was set up in the corner and Mr. Hampton was preoccupied with the enormous mass he was bench-pressing. The students watched for a few moments, mesmerized by the display of shear muscle.

"Mr. Hampton?" Connor interrupted. "Team Two is here for our briefing."

The tremendous kilograms of weight were gently lowered back down on the stack. The hulk of a man sat up and reached for his towel. Without saying a word, he stood up and headed for his office patting himself with his towel.

The students, except for Doug, followed closely behind. Doug walked up to the bench press, grabbed a hold of one of the grips, and heaved. The stack remained unmoved.

"You should give up on that karate stuff and join us in weight lifting, Doug," Mr. Hampton stated without turning around.

Molly looked back at Doug. His face went red.

When everyone was seated at the table in Mr. Hampton's spacious office, he began. "I understand Beth has filled you all in on the basics of your assignments."

They all nodded.

"Good. Let's move onto the actual mission parameters. This is a short undertaking that shouldn't last for more than about three hours. We are flying you down tomorrow afternoon. From the airport, we will take you to this site. It's about three miles from the building." He pointed to a map he laid out on the table at the onset of the meeting.

"We will have six BMX bikes ready for you. You are to pose as a group of kids out for a bike ride. You'll just be curious about the building you come across. Any questions, so far?" He paused to allow them the chance to ask. No one offered a question, so he continued.

"The four of you," he said, pointing to Connor, Doug, Julie, and Beth, "will conduct the actual surveillance. Matt and Molly, you will stay back here near the other's bikes," again pointing on the map.

"The four of you might have the best luck entering the building at this point. SYLVIA will assist you through your SPAs. I'm sure Raymond . . . Mr. Dunston has some kind of security locks on the doors. It's probably going to be a lot like the ones used on the Egyptian Embassy in Berlin last year, Connor."

They all looked at Connor as he recalled the ALPHA/NUMERIC pad. "I remember. It didn't take SYLVIA long to get me the passcode."

"How do you know the type of security the building would have?" Molly asked.

Before Mr. Hampton could answer Beth spoke up, "Dunston designed it for them. It's his most advanced security system."

"That's correct, Beth. You're going to be a big help on this assignment."

"You think there are going to be problems, Mr. Hampton?"

The big man looked down toward Julie. "I don't know. Quite honestly, no one knows what you're going to find there. If we take Dunston on his word, it's just a power transfer site. But no one around here thinks much of Dunston's word."

Thoughts traveled through each of their minds. If it wasn't what he said it was, then what was it? Connor recalled other assignments when advanced intelligence wasn't correct. He already had his share of surprises in the past. The advantage of being a team of kids was the "innocent factor." More times than not he and his team escaped out of tight situations just by falling back on being annoying or snooping kids. When ruthless individuals would run across a few kids meddling around the last thought they ever had was espionage. This was what Mr. McMichael always called visible-stealth. People always assume things based on prior knowledge or prior exposure and both have taught that grown-ups are the ones in harms way, not kids.

"What are we packing?" Doug asked.

"That's where I was going next. We want you all, except Molly and Matt, to have palm stunners and of course everyone will have SPAs. The four of you going in the building are to have com-buds."

Connor looked over to Matt and Molly and explained palm stunners as palmed devices that stun any person by tapping them with the stunner. Doug pointed out that they also work on attacking Doberman pinchers.

Molly looked at Matt and explained, "Com-buds are small devices that fit inside an ear, and they look like small hearing aids. They transmit the sounds around the other team members. If someone is separated from the team and is having a conversation with another person, the entire team can hear the discussion."

Connor looked suspiciously at his little sister. Beth winked at her.

"They also have channels," Mr. Hunter added, also looking at Molly apprehensively. He turned to Matt and continued, "If you tap your ear you can change from the entire group to an individual. Plus, you can send messages from one person to another just by talking."

"Another nice feature is the one-on-one conversations you can have," Doug said, looking at

Julie. "If you both have it set for one channel then only that person picks up your communications."

"How do you know who's on which channel?" Matt asked.

"Easy," Julie explained. "It goes by age: Connor, Beth, Doug, me. If you're talking to Connor and you want to talk to Doug next, that would be two more taps. Two taps again gets you back to the whole group."

"Interesting," Matt said, scratching his chin.

Mr. Hunter covered a few more details with the group and answered any questions anyone had. The departure time was set for 1:30 in the afternoon. Everyone left the gym-office looking forward to the mission. Connor told Matt and Molly that every assignment was exciting. He had been on more operations than he could remember and when a new one started, it was like the first one all over again.

Chapter Twelve
"Hi, Matt. What's new?"
– Joey

The team decided to stop at the armory before splitting up for the night. They wanted to show Matt and Molly the palm stunners and com-buds. Matt was awed by the display of gadgets in the room. He enjoyed looking at the 3D digital cameras and translator com-buds. Connor picked up a sphere-shaped object that he explained was a camera. It could be rolled across a room taking video as it rolled. SYLVIA kept track of the ball's rotation and thirteen separate cameras, then assembled an incredibly detailed 360-degree image of the room. Conner recalled for Matt. He explained using one on two different assignments. One was during a fire. He had to toss the ball through the flames and allow it roll beyond the fire so they could see what was on the other side. It helped save the vice president's daughter from being kidnapped two years ago. Matt was incredibly impressed.

He asked Connor what stops someone from walking out of the room with anything, since no one but them was present. Connor explained that each item was linked to SYLVIA. Someone would have to shut SYLVIA down in order to take anything. Further, he explained, still holding the silver ball, "Try to leave the room." Matt walked to the door and pulled at the handle. It was locked tight. After Connor put the ball back down, Matt tried the door again; this time it opened easily.

"SYLVIA locks the room if any item is picked up and not signed out," Conner explained. He gestured to a pedestal with a green thumb pad near the door. Matt reasoned one must press it with the item in order to sign it out.

Doug showed Molly and Matt a pair of palm scanners. They tried them on. He explained how placing the thumb on your index finger between the last two knuckles activated them. "This is not a normal position for your hand so you don't need to worry about accidentally turning it on," he clarified.

"If you want to try it out you can use it on Connor," Doug chided.

"I don't think so!" Connor responded with a laugh.

Matt looked at the device in his palm. It looked like a glove that had lost its fingers and most of its back. "What does it feel like?"

"It causes a tingling feeling throughout your entire body and then you go completely limp," Julie explained. "The effect lasts for only about ten minutes, and then you regain all muscle movement again."

"You'll get your chance to try one out firsthand in Mr. Hampton's PE class. He lets you stun students," Beth told them.

"But don't worry," Doug added, "someone will get to stun you of course."

The group looked at the com-bud, then the tour ended and the three boys bid the three girls good night. They all went back to their rooms.

Placed neatly on the beds, when the boys entered their room, was their mail. Connor received two letters, one of them from his mother. Doug found a letter from his parents and his copy of *Outdoor Life* magazine. To Matt's surprise, his SPA indicated an e-mail letter had arrived. Each boy went straight to his mail and began reading.

Matt called up his letter.

Hi, Matt.

I hope everything is going well for you. It's been really strange since you left. Those two men that stayed behind arranged new foster homes for all of us.

Mrs. Helmut is not doing foster care anymore. They told us she has a new job, but wouldn't tell us what it was.

I went to a house in Fort Lauderdale that same day. Nice foster parents. They gave me my own room and we had pizza the first night. It was my pick.

Then the best thing ever happened. A nice couple came in yesterday and met me. We talked for a while and then I went for a ride with them. We went to a pizza place that has these video games. I got pizza again and I got to play all the video games I wanted. (I wasn't very good at them.)

They told me they're going to come back on Saturday and I might get to go home with them for the weekend. They have a dog and big house and a big yard. I hope they don't want me to weed their gardens or anything. (Ha ha.)

Matt, this might be the real thing. I might get adopted, finally. I'm so excited. Of all the foster kids in the world, they might pick me!

I hope your school is going well and you're making good friends. All the boys at the old foster home said it was you that set us free. You sure are lucky. Thanks, Matt.

Your friend,
Joey

Howell, MR.   Wesley-Hampton Academy

Matt stared at the letter on the screen and recalled a few days ago when the rains came down and he was swept away on a tidal wave. He watched as water splashed on "Fort Lauderdale," creating a small pool. Except it wasn't. He could feel another tear moving down his cheek and wiped it away. Without thinking it through or saying anything to his roommates, he dashed from his bed and left the room.

Doug looked up from his magazine as the door to the room shut hard behind Matt. "I wonder what that's all about."

"Beats me," Connor said and continued reading his letter.

Matt wandered the halls for a while and stopped at the library. He plopped down on one of the comfortable leather chairs in the center of the room and reread his letter. For quite a while he sat there and wondered what might have happened if he had stayed. It might have been him that someone would be looking at to adopt right now. He could have parents, a family, and a big house. He felt anger at Joey begin to grow inside of him as he thought about his best friend falling into such incredible good fortune.

"Matt are you alright?" a concerned voice interrupted his thoughts.

He looked up and saw Molly standing next to him. She wore a white robe over her blue pajamas and a pair of bunny slippers on her feet. "I couldn't sleep so I went for a walk. I guess I'm more nervous than I thought. You too?"

Words didn't want to come out of his mouth. He was still absorbed in the letter and talking with anyone was the last thing he wanted. However, it appeared he had little choice in the situation as he watched Molly get comfortable in a chair facing his.

She noticed his moist green eyes and the SPA he clenched tightly in his hand. She looked away from his eyes and down to the device. "Is that an e-mail?" She nodded toward his hands. "Do you want to talk about it?"

"It's nobody you know."

"Well, I knew that," she said, breaking the ice.

Matt chuckled and looked at her. He knew she could tell he had been crying, but it didn't seem to bother her. She pushed back her auburn hair and smiled. He handed her the gadget. "It's from my best friend, Joey. He and I were at the same foster home."

Cautiously, she took hold of the letter. Matt was reluctant to let go and she was not about to pull it away. Finally, he let go and she drew it closer. She silently read the communication.

"Wow! He sure is lucky."

"Yeah," Matt mumbled, taking back his SPA. "He sure is."

It took Molly a moment to put the pieces together, but when she did, the picture was completely clear. "You wish that was you, don't you?"

"Of course I do. Every kid in foster care looks forward to the day when they can call someone mom or dad. You go to bed thinking about it and you wake up thinking about it."

Molly listened and knew she had nothing comforting to say. She wasn't sure if she could even relate, but she could defend Joey. "It's not Joey's fault he might get a family. You should be happy for him."

There was a silence while the words settled into Matt's head. She was right and he knew it. It wasn't Joey's fault. "I am happy for him," he confessed.

"Look, Matt. You're here and he's there. He's making the best of his situation and I'm sure you'll do the same. You're incredibly smart. You're probably the smartest kid I know."

Matt remembered Joey saying the same thing to him the day he left and it made him smile.

"You were blowing us all away in the computer room. Even Mr. St. Lucia was impressed. Why do you think Mr. McMichael brought you here? Besides, parents are overrated."

"That's easy for you to say. You've got a mom."

"Sort of. She really wasn't around much while we were growing up. I learned to do a lot on my own."

"But you *have* a mom. You have someone that you can go to when you need to. Someone who will say, 'I knew you would do that' or pat you on the back when you do something great. Or someone who appreciates you for who you are. You've got that; I might never."

Molly looked deep into his moist green eyes. "When I decided to come here, I left all that behind. Sure, my mom is important to me; I can't deny that. But there's more to me than having a mom. I came here to expand on who I am and to make a difference in this world. My mom will continue to be my mom all the time I'm here. I'll continue to get letters from her and I'll continue to write her back." Her eyes grazed on a shelf of books in the distance and then returned her gaze on Matt's eyes. "I want to be who I make myself to be, not what someone else wants me to be."

Matt intently listened and realized she made a lot of sense. He looked away and focused on a philodendron growing in a mauve pot near a display of Turkish swords. He couldn't predict the future; the last several days showed that all too clearly, but he could alter the future. He could make a difference in this world too. When he looked back a Molly, she was handing him tissues. He wiped his eyes and thanked her.

"You're going to make a great difference here, Matt. I just know it. And tomorrow is going to be our first mission."

Matt laughed. "Yeah, some mission. We get to go bike riding."

"Hey, it's a start!"

"It's a great start!" came a voice.

They both were startled at finding Mr. McMichael standing near them. "But if you don't get to bed you'll end up sleeping through the entire mission."

The two students jumped up and started heading for the door.

"About tomorrow," Mr. McMichael said, causing the two to stop and turn around. "Be ready for anything. I don't trust Raymond Dunston. He's hiding something. This is too small for him."

They both looked at him blankly.

"Just be ready. If we are all lucky, all this will be is a bike ride. And if we're not, it could be our last bike ride. I trust you two, and so does your team. You will do well. Now head to bed; it's a big day tomorrow."

Howell, MR.   Wesley-Hampton Academy

Chapter Thirteen
"Turning around now would only set us back a day." – Connor

Breakfast was quiet. Mr. McMichael explained to the students what was happening later in the day. He told them about Team Two's task and of Beth's temporary assignment. He also told everyone another weather anomaly had occurred late last night. A line of thunderstorms near Memphis had produced several category 4 and 5 tornados. Like the other events, this one was not moving far either. He told them that the six storms had caused thirty-six deaths and hospitalized hundreds as of this morning. Matt noticed the concern in Mr. McMicheal's voice.

Everyone ate quietly.

Later that morning, the team was driven to the Boston Airport where they boarded a jet similar to the kind Matt rode on his way to Wesley-Hampton Academy. They departed on a private runway away from all the commercial flights.

Everything moved along as planned. The team arrived at Dallas and rode to the site where they would begin their three-mile bike ride. The drivers of the Dodge Durango said nothing. Matt wondered if they knew anything about the plans. He figured they must be part of the transportation used by the school since most of the students weren't licensed drivers. Butterflies performed cartwheels in Matt's stomach. As they rode, they all sat quietly. Connor read his e-mail on his SPA and Doug helped Julie solve a math problem. When Matt looked over at Beth, it appeared to him that she was taking a nap. Molly smiled at him. He was sure she was as nervous as he was, but her calm demeanor didn't show it.

The vehicle parked near a thicket of cedar. Six bikes lay on the grass near one of the gangly trees. The team filed out of both sides of the minivan and formed a circle. Connor began a last-minute briefing, answering all the questions anyone had. The four veterans checked the batteries in their palm stunners and fastened them to their hands.

Molly watched the others switch on their com-buds and test them out. Matt pulled out his SPA and pulled up the letter written by Dunston, stored in SYLVIA's memory, and read it over. Something kept calling out to him from within the note.

Seeing potential break in their conversation, Matt said, "You know there's something strange about this letter." He looked back at his SPA screen with the letter.

The four other students moved behind Matt and read at the letter. "We've been over this letter a hundred times," Beth told him. "The entire thing is strange. Why even leave a note, other than to try and keep us away."

"That's not the strange part I'm talking about. What bothers me is the part about the power transfer. How does he transfer the power? I mean, where does it go?"

They all examined the letter as if it would answer their question. "To another building," Doug answered curtly.

"No, Doug, it can't. There would need to be wires or conduits running somewhere else. And nothing in the satellite photos showed any cables leaving the building."

"So?" Doug said, baiting him to explain.

Beth tilted her head. "Matt's right. To transfer the power from one site to another would involve some kind of wires. He could have never run the wires very far. They would have to go for miles. And that would take them across other people's property."

"Or state lines," Matt added. "Especially if he has more power transfer sites spread around. They would all have to be wired to the main building."

Connor thought about everything for a moment and then looked up in the direction of the building, as if he could actually see it from that distance. "We might be riding into a trap."

"This might be the only building Dunston has anywhere!"

"That's exactly what I was thinking, Doug," Connor said, mulling over his options.

"What are you thinking, Connor?" Beth asked.

Connor took a couple seconds more to think before answering. "The way I see it, we need to continue the mission. Time is not on our side right now. Dunston is going to continue his manipulation of the weather if we don't do something."

"If we don't continue, Mr. McMichael will just send another team in and we'll have wasted perhaps an entire day," Beth added.

"I agree," Doug concurred.

"Do you think we need to contact Mr. McMichael?" Julie asked.

"Not yet," Connor told her. "We can't jump to conclusions. That would be hasty. Besides, we all agree, if we turn around now he'll just send in another team. Why couldn't that just *be* us?"

Without another word, the six mounted their bikes and headed out in search of the building.

The ride itself was not more than thirty minutes. They located the place where Mr. Hunter told them to keep the bikes. Connor, Beth, Doug, and Julie dismounted and gathered for a final equipment check. Molly and Matt waited for a couple minutes before leaving their bikes on the grass. They watched their teammates prepare for their investigation of the structure.

"Matt, Molly, you two will be able to watch our progress on your SPAs. Each of us will have our videos on so you will be able to see everything our SPAs see," Connor told them. He showed them how to split their screens into four small monitors, one for each of the investigating team's cameras. They could see what the recording lens on the leading edge of each SPA picked up.   SYLVIA would also get a video feed and provide the staff at Wesley-Hampton something to monitor back at the school.

With everything taken care of, Connor beckoned his team with a wave of his arm. "Let's roll!"

Molly and Matt watched them move away into the distance.

Matt looked down at his SPA and saw the four separate images. He looked at the one labeled "DOUG." It showed Connor in front of him and the building growing larger.

When they reached the door of the building, Matt switched to Connor's full view. The view from Connor's SPA filled his screen. He saw the touch pad that his teammates carefully examined. A series of numbers and letters appeared at the bottom of the screen. Each of the twelve symbols changed rapidly. One by one, the rotating stopped and from left to right the pass code to the building appeared: A-F-4-G-X-J-4-Y-M-9-8-Q.

"Oh. That's the code. We could have guessed that," Molly said, laughing sarcastically.

They switched back to the four separate images and watched them move into the building. One by one, each of the four quadrants went blank.

"That's odd," Matt said. "They all shut off their cameras."

"Connor never said anything about that, did he?"

Matt shook his head, still watching his blank device.

Chapter Fourteen
"The difference between a fly in a spider's web and you is the fly isn't used as bait."
– A voice in the hallway

Julie was the last in the building and the first to turn around as the door closed behind them. She instinctively pulled on the handle. It was locked. Each of them felt a little uneasy.

"I wonder if it shut on its own accord," Connor said in a low voice.

"Or someone else's accord," Doug added.

The four adventurers looked around. They found themselves in a long, quiet hallway that ran, what looked to be, the length of the building. Doors could be spotted punctuating the walls at various positions down the hall. Everything was white except the carpet. It was a shade of jade.

Connor looked at the others as his fingers moved over the top of his SPA. With practiced precision he pressed all of the right buttons to send a message to Mr. McMichael.

The silence was broken with a sound none of them wanted to hear. It startled them. "Go ahead, Connor, press all the buttons you want. It will do you no good." The voice was, without a doubt, male and confident and knew they were there. "These outer walls were designed to specifically stop the communications from a SPA."

Beth passed a worried glance in Connor's direction. He called Connor by name and knew of SPAs. She did not like the way this was heading; it could only be one person.

"Don't look so surprised, everyone. Come now, you must have expected some type of welcome."

Connor's mind churned as fast as Beth's and he, too, added the facts correctly. "Dunston!"

"Very good, Connor. But I'm not overly impressed."

"How do you know my name?"

"That's easy. It's being sent from your SPA. I was notified of your presence as soon as that tin box of a computer cycled through pass codes."

"But, you said . . ."

"I can see McMichael is not teaching you to listen very well. I said your signals couldn't *leave* this building. Your little useless toys are not going to help you in here, but they have helped me."

"You are going to let us go, aren't you?"

"Not very likely. Besides, this is the safest place to be right now." There was a hint of laughter at the end of the last sentence.

The three captives looked at their leader for advice. All they got was a shrug from his shoulders.

The voice continued. "Here is what I want you to do. Down the hall to the left is a series of doors. I will unlock the fourth one. I want the four of you to please walk down there and have a seat. I will be there shortly. Help yourself to something to drink while you wait."

"You mean make ourselves at home?" Doug asked.

There was no reply.

"Doug, this would not be a great time to get him mad," Julie explained.

As the foursome headed down the hall, Connor turned and looked back. He was sure he had heard a couple of clicking noises, but there was nothing there.

They reached the door and Julie opened it up. When she stepped inside the lights came on and revealed a large room. In the center of the room was an enormous oak table with comfortable chairs placed around at twelve different locations. Each spot at the table housed a microphone, a glass for water, and a folder.

Doug walked up to the conference table and looked at one of the folders. They were all white with the words "DUNSTON LABS" in bold red script across the middle. Inside he found several pages of text, all written in Arabic. There were drawings, charts, and diagrams. Nothing he could read.

"It's all in Arabic," he told the others.

They each walked up to the table and opened a folder near them.

"Not this one," Beth said. "It's in French." They all looked at her while she scanned the paper. Her face lost all color. She brought her hand up to her mouth and said softly, "Oh, my gosh!"

. . .

Matt and Molly stared at the SPA screen, waiting for an image to reappear. It stayed black. The two looked at each other. There was no way of knowing what their teammates were encountering in the silent building. From their poor vantage point, they could not even imagine the trouble the four were in.

"It's been ten minutes. I'm sure everything is going well in there, Matt," Molly said with very little conviction in her voice.

"You don't sound like you mean it."

"Well, they probably know what they're doing. They've been doing this kind of thing longer than us."

"That doesn't mean there isn't any trouble," Matt said as his SPA image changed. "Look at this."

The two looked at the message that appeared on his screen.

"*We have lost contact with the investigating team. They may have walked into a trap. We are sending the vehicles in to pick the two of you up. Stay where you are. McMichael.*"

Neither Matt nor Molly knew what to say. They looked briefly at each other and then back to the screen.

. . .

Beth set the paper back down on the open folder at the same moment the door opened. All four of the students spun around, and Beth lowered her hand from her mouth.

"You monster!" she yelled out. "How could you?"

The tall, slender man walked into the room. His hair was a blend between gray and black and was trimmed short. A similar colored beard cut its way across his face, and an aged scar was noticeable below his right eye.   He looked like a distinguished yet weathered man.

He smiled at Beth. "Those were very well thought out words, thank you. Are you Beth or Julie?"

"How can you do this?" They all looked at Beth confused. "Have you no decency?"

"On the contrary, I am full of decency. You are all alive, aren't you?"

"What's this all about, Beth?" Connor asked, walking over to her.

"Ah! Beth. And you must be Connor. I recognized your voice. That makes you Doug, the smart aleck, and you must be Julie. My name is Raymond Dunston, your host."

"Your international murderer is more like it," Beth spat.

"Beth, you need to calm down," Connor told her in a soothing tone.

She looked at Connor for a moment and turned to Dunston. "Tell them your plan."

"Impetuous, aren't we? I would love to share my plan with you all. But first I have a little business to take care of. Have a seat."

The four sat down and watched Dunston. He walked up to the table and pressed a button.

"Yes, sir."

"Ralph, would you initiate weather cycle 'Wesley-Hampton' for me?"

"Yes, sir." There was a pause. "Initiated, sir. Is there anything else?"

"No, Ralph. Just monitor it. There shouldn't be any more interruptions." He pressed the button again and sat down. "It gets a little bumpy for a moment," he told them, placing his elbows on the table and resting his head on his hands.

A humming sound surrounded them as they each looked around for the source. The sound grew louder and the glasses on the table began to shake. They could feel the entire building shutter for a couple of moments and then stop and everything settled back to normal.

"That was just a transfer of power," he told them. "Nothing to worry about. At least not here anyway."

"What did you do to our school?" Julie asked sternly.

The poised man smiled. "Nothing less than your McMichael wanted. I told him not to interfere."

Doug shot up from his chair. "You're going to harm innocent people just so you can play with the weather. Those student's lives are worth more than this little game of yours!"

"It's not a little game, Doug. It's bigger than you can imagine and this butcher is going to walk away with more than one hundred trillion dollars times twelve."

Dunston smiled. "I like you Beth. You're fun."

Chapter Fifteen
"Having power, control, and money is so underrated."
– Raymond Dunston

Molly covered her ears as the humming sound vibrating from the building reached deafening levels. In a matter of a few seconds it stopped.

Matt still felt the ringing in his ears as he removed his hands.

"That must have been another transfer of power," he told her.

"Whatever it was, it was loud. I hope they're alright in there."

For the second time in as many minutes a message from Mr. McMichael appeared.

The message scrolled across Matt's SPA. It was choppy, but the two were able to piece it together:

"Can't   ...   vehicle...wind   and   light...   our way...doesn't... good here...do the be... you can. We are coun... on you...Good Lu..."

"They're getting hit with a strong lightning storm it sounds like," Molly explained.

"Yeah. He wants us to do something."

"What do you have in mind, Matt?"

The dark-haired boy thought for a moment. The way he saw it there was only one option: enter the building and go after their teammates. It wasn't the option he wanted, but it was the only option they had to pick from. "We're going in."

"How? We can't get SYLVIA to break the code anymore. We've lost contact with the school."

"We don't need SYLVIA. She's already given us everything we need to get in." Matt pressed a couple of the buttons around the SPA screen and the saved image from Connor's SPA appeared. The pass code to the building was back on Matt's screen.

"Yes!" Molly exclaimed.

"Let's go, Molly. We have friends to rescue and a school to save."

Molly grabbed his arm. "I hope we're not too late. I hope we can make a difference."

Matt remembered Joey grabbing his arm as they left the basement furnace. He left his safe confines and ventured into uncharted waters. Now he was doing it again. Only this time he felt surer of himself. He felt compelled to move ahead and it felt good. Matt could only think of his new friends in the building and everyone at the school. For the first time in his life, he felt like a part of a family and there was no way he was going to let that feeling get away. He had finally come home.

The two raced across the barren landscape to the door where their teammates vanished. Matt looked at the keypad and took a long slow breath. Slowly he pressed the code as Molly read it from the screen. The last entry was pressed and the two heard a click from the door. They looked at the knob for a moment and Matt reached out and slowly turned it. He pulled the door open and they entered the building.

Everything was as quiet as it was for the previous visitors. The door slowly closed behind them. Molly examined her SPA and saw the images from the other four displayed on hers again. She showed Matt. His, too, showed the quarter display.

The four views were similar to each other. They looked to be lying on a table in a pile. A couple of the views showed edges of the other SPAs. They displayed a chair and a wall. There was no sign of anyone.

"I think we need to be very careful," Matt said. "I'm not sure why they are separated from their SPAs."

Matt glanced over to Molly who looked equally confused. She tried to send a message to Mr. McMichael, but it appeared not to send.

"Something in these walls is preventing the signal from getting out," Matt reasoned.

"So we have to do this without any help, even from SYLVIA," Molly agreed.

Matt started down the hallway looking at all the doors. He decided they would need to check each one in the hope of finding their friends. When all of a sudden he stopped. There was something small on the ground that he had kicked further down the hall.

He listened to the sound of the object bounce several times across the floor and come to rest. His eyes focused in on the direction of the sound and soon spied the item. Matt walked a few paces forward and picked it up. It was a com-bud.

"Molly, look at this!" he exclaimed with a muted voice, holding up the treasure.

"Who's do you think it is?" Molly pondered.

"I don't know. Let's see if it even works anymore."

Matt inserted the device in his ear and a conversation came to life. He listened for a moment, hearing all the voices in the room. Only one he didn't recognize.

He cupped his hand over his ear and whispered to Molly, "I'm picking up their voices. They sound okay, but there is someone else in the room talking to them."

"What are they talking about?"

Matt held up one finger toward Molly and she let him listen.

"It's not a little game, Doug. It's bigger than you can imagine and this butcher is going to walk away with more than one hundred trillion dollars times twelve."

"I like you Beth. You're fun."

"I don't understand," Connor said. "What's one hundred trillion dollars?" He looked at Dunston.

"Well, I don't see any reason not to tell you. It not like you can stop me now," he laughed. "This building you're in is the only one I have. It was designed to create any weather anomaly I choose. Plus I can place it anywhere I want."

Matt could not see Dunston press a button on the table and activate a weather map on the screen behind him. "If you notice, the Boston area is presently witnessing a horrific storm right now: lightning, winds, and hail. It's quite spectacular. Of course, it will worsen before it gets better. The best is yet to come.

I've programmed four tornadoes to hit your little school in the next hour."

Each of the students gasped at the sight on the map and the vision each possessed in their heads. They were helpless while their friends were in peril.

"That's not the worst of it," Beth told them. "He's has no regard for human life!"

"Now, Beth. That hurts. And we've had such a great friendship."

"He's taking this whole storm thing globally." She picked up the folder in front her and tossed it into the center of the table. "He's buying leaders of other countries and providing them the weather of their choice."

"You're going to destroy the world's economy for money?" Doug asked in horror.

Matt could not see the wicked smile spreading across Raymond Dunston's face, but he could hear the evil in his voice. "You couldn't be more wrong! I could care less about the world's economy."

"But you said . . ." Julie started.

"I lied! There's no money in controlling tourism, but there's plenty of money in war!"

"War!" Connor burst out.

Dunston looked at him skeptically. "Yes, war. Imagine if you could have perfect weather while you prepare your troops and your enemy gets foul weather. Why risk the lives of your soldiers when a tornado could be more efficient."

Julie tapped her ear as she listened to voices from her com-bud. She cycled through the team and isolated the signal from Beth's earpiece, but not from Beth. Julie listened as Matt explained what he received, and she heard Molly gasp.

Dunston revealed the meeting that was to begin in four hours. There were representatives from twelve different countries attending, all bringing their funds to the meeting. Julie caught Beth's eye and pointed to her ear. She mouthed the name Matt to her. Beth understood and winked.

"So, if you don't mind me asking, did you want us to come down the hall to this room to tell us all this?" Julie asked.

Matt listened to Dunston's affirmative answer and looked down the hallway. He saw a light coming from a room whose door was ajar. "They're in there," he told Molly.

"I don't suggest going that way." She pressed a couple of buttons on her SPA and the map SYLVIA created the day before appeared. "It looks like a large room is behind that door," she told him.

The two walked a couple of steps down the hall and stopped at the white metal door. Matt slowly pulled down on the handle and the door opened. They slipped quietly inside and the lights turned on.

Molly and Matt stood stunned at the layout of the room. From the large gray cabinets to the blue sparkling tank it was exactly like the computer room at Wesley-Hampton Academy.

"This is SYLVIA's same room," Molly said. "How could Dunston have the same computer?"

Matt walked around the room for a moment. "Something's different. Something's not the same." He approached the computer screen and stared at the image of the United States. All the present storms were visible. The system in Florida and the two in California were gone. He looked toward Boston. A mass of blue and green was fixed just south of the city.

"That's where the school is," he said pointing. "We have got to stop that storm somehow."

Matt sat down at the keyboard and pressed ENTER. Nothing changed on the massive screen. "How do I get this map off the screen?"

"*What would you like to see?*" Said a voice from the ceiling. It was a male voice with a slight southern drawl. Matt and Molly looked at each other. *We're caught,* they thought simultaneously.

The two made no sounds for nearly a minute. The hum from the computer's processors comprised the only sound in the room. In Matt's ear he could still hear the conversation with Dunston and his team. They continue to talk about manipulating the weather. Then the question came again. *"What would you like to see?"*

Molly quietly walked up to the back of Matt's chair and said, "Are you the computer?"

"I would prefer to have you call me SHERMAN."

Molly let out her breath in relief.

"SHERMAN, could you display a list of your commands that deal with the weather machine?"

Matt stared in delight as a list of fifteen commands appeared on the screen. Most of them had a "+" in front of them and three had 🔒. He assumed the plus opened up new levels with additional subcommands and the symbol 🔒 meant locked or password protected. The three with the locked symbol were: Initiate Storm, Terminate Storm, and System Shutdown.

He moved the mouse across the screen and clicked on "System Shutdown." A small blue box appeared on the screen asking for a password. Matt slammed his fist on the table.

"SHERMAN, could you tell us the password?" Molly asked.

"I'm sorry, that level information is protected."

"It was worth a try," she told Matt. He smiled sympathetically.

Matt looked intently at the list of commands. Was there something he was missing? The two commands that had any power were blocked from use. He studied the remaining orders. They were grouped in categories: Maps, location, intensity, duration, type, and size.

"How about intensity," Molly suggested. "Maybe we could lower the strength of the storm."

"It's worth a try."

Matt clicked on the "+" next to intensity. A short list appeared. Increase, decrease, and terminate storm were the choices. Terminate had 🔒 in front of it and was quickly ruled out, leaving decrease as their only hope. Matt double clicked.

"All commands for the present storm must be activated from the Storm Control Center."

Matt looked at Molly. "SHERMAN, could you show us a layout of the building?"

A plan of the building was displayed on the screen.

"Would you like it downloaded to your SPAs?"

Neither of the two answered. Molly mouthed the letters S-P-A to Matt.

Howell, MR.   Wesley-Hampton Academy

Slowly and thoughtfully Matt asked, "SHERMAN, what's an SPA?"

"SHERMAN'S   PERSONNEL ASSISTANT."

"You can connect to our SPAs? Who built you?" Matt asked.

"Yes, I can. Dunston Labs built me. Would you like more information?"

Matt and Molly's eyes opened wide and locked on one another. Perhaps there was hope after all.

Chapter Sixteen
"What! I have a sister?"
– SHERMAN

Matt told the computer they wanted to know more.

"I was completed in March of 2003. Raymond Dunston added my final memory core on December14th, 2005. There has not been a significant upgrade since then.   I am the only computer in the world capable of processing at my present speed and maintaining a working LCD tank."

Matt chuckled. "What if I told you that you had an older sister?"

"I'm not capable of having a sibling."

"Matt, we're using too much time here. If we need to get to the control center we better hurry."

Matt agreed and turned back to the screen. "SHERMAN, download the image to our SPAs and show us the fastest route to the Control Center."

Matt and Molly looked at the map on the big screen. A dotted red line ran from the computer room, down a hallway, and stopped at a room half the size of the one they were standing in. The hallway leading to the room was not the one they came in from earlier. Matt felt relieved that he did not have to walk past the room with Dunston in it. If his teammates could keep him busy, they could easily take care of business in the control room.

"SHERMAN, how many people are in the building right now?" Matt asked.

"There are presently eight people. I only know the names of two of them. Would you like to see where they are?"

Matt and Molly both said yes at the same time and SHERMAN added small figurines to the map. Five figures were represented in one room. One was labeled "R. Dunston"; the remaining four had no labels. Two figures depicted Matt and Molly, and much to Matt's dismay, one figure labeled "R. Samson" moved about in the Control Center.

"Well, there goes easy," Matt declared.

The two made their way down the hall as quickly as possible. Knowing where everyone was at made it easier to move through the building stealthily. Silence wasn't necessary; speed was.

They reached the door of the control room and peered in the window. Seated with his back to them was a man in his late thirties. His shaved head stared at the computer screen in front of him. He studied the image of the storm raging havoc on the Atlantic costal city.

"We need a plan, Molly," Matt whispered.

"I wish we had a palm stunner. It would make things a lot easier.

"I don't think I can do much one-on-one with this guy. We're going to have to team up on him."

"I think you can leave this guy to me," Molly said. She grabbed each of her wrists and swung her arms left and right stretching her torso muscles. Next, she reached behind herself and pulled her ankles up one at a time.

"Do you know how to fight or something?"

"I've been in a few," she admitted with a shy grin. She removed her shoes and socks and stood on her toes. Matt heard her ankles crack as she rose up and slowly came back down.

"Well, here goes. This should be fun."

Matt detected not a hint of nervousness in her voice. He had the feeling she was not hiding anything; she had complete confidence in her skills. Slowly and furtively, she opened the door and entered the room. Her plan was to simply sneak up behind him and render him unconscious with one strike.

She knew her plan would have worked if only she could have had the opportunity to use it. As soon as she stepped away from the door, the man turned in his seat.

A confused look was carved across his face. It was obvious this was not a common occurrence. "Who are you, and how did you get in here?"

Molly's element of surprise dissipated. She stopped, planted her feet shoulder width apart, and drew her hands up in front of her. Her fingers were spread apart and bent slightly forward, thumbs tucked in out of the way. She stood ready for any possible attack, anything except the yellow button.

The man sized up the situation and then leaned over to a yellow button and pressed it. "Sir, there is a little red-haired girl standing in your control room. Did you send her here?"

Molly wanted anything but that last announcement. Why couldn't he have just attacked like anyone else? She broke her stance and ran directly at the man.

With his body leaning toward the panel of buttons, he found himself in an awkward position to defend himself. As the young girl raced toward him, he fumbled with different options in his mind. Only one looked best to him. As Molly neared him, he kicked the chair he was previously sitting in toward her. The chair easily coasted across the laminate floor in the direction of the sprinting youth.

Without slowing down, Molly jumped into the air; she drew her left leg to her chest and extended her right leg at a right angle aimed directly at the man's chest. The chair rolled past her, beneath her. As she floated in her seated position, her victim could only watch. Molly quickly, and with perfect timing, switched positions of her legs. Her left foot smashed against the man's chest as her right leg recoiled to her chest.

The man shot backwards and bounced off a panel of cabinet doors. He fell face-first to the floor. Molly stood in her original position looking intently at the motionless body.

Matt burst into the room. "That was incredible, Molly."

"That was not the way I had it planned. He called Dunston."

Matt moved his hand to his ear. "Julie just said Dunston's on his way. She said he looked mad."

"SHERMAN, lock the control room doors," Molly yelled out, standing up straight and dropping her arms.

The sound of locks audibly clicked. "Where's the control station?" Matt asked. He looked around and spotted the weather map on a screen across the room. Quickly he ran over and requested SHERMAN to pull up the commands again.

"You figure out how to stop the storm; I'll hold off Dunston," Molly directed, facing the door in her attack posture. She knew the locks were not going to stop him, only slow him down.

Chapter Seventeen
"You certainly didn't learn those moves
at Wesley-Hampton Academy."
– Dunston

Matt hastily went to work at the computer, pulling up the decrease command. He clicked on the command. His breath was knocked completely out of him as if the blue box on the screen had actually punched him.

He read it. Decrease function only valid during storm set-up.

He stared at the remaining commands as he heard the locks around the room click free.

"Here we go, Matt," Molly shouted out as the door busted open.

"How did you get in here?" the bearded man hollered. "What happened to Ralph?" He was relieved to see him still breathing and only unconscious.

Dunston turned his attention to the figure standing ten feet away and looking intense. "Well, old McMichael sure pulled one over on me. I didn't expect a second team from him. First the big kids and then the overzealous little kids. Is there a third team in pull-ups somewhere?"

Dunston ignored Molly. "SHERMAN, how many people are in the building right now?"

"There are two groups of people in the building. Four unknown people are locked in conference room 18b and you, Ralph Sampson, Matthew Malone, and an unknown person are in the control room."

Dunston stood with a confused look on his face. He tilted his head to the left slightly and said, "SHERMAN, would you please repeat that last answer?"

The computer began its last statement, *"There are two groups in the building. Four unknown people are locked in conference room . . . "*

Dunston never had the chance to hear the rest of the answer, for at that moment he found himself flying backwards. Molly's foot launched into his chest and the rest of his body went airborne, crashing into the door behind him. His body slid down to the ground.

Molly thought it was too easy. She felt as if there should have been a little resistance as she watched Dunston spring from the ground like he was made of rubber. *Be careful what you wish for*, she scolded herself.

Dunston completed his rebound and stood ready to fight. Molly, likewise, planted her feet at shoulder width, raised her hands in front of her body, palms out and thumbs tucked in. A look of complete composure spread across her entire body.

"Karate," Dunston said. "Are they still teaching that at Wesley-Hampton? That was my old subject."

Molly did not respond.

"I'm sure it's gone downhill since I was there. I would have to guess, by your age, you've probably reached orange belt by now." He smiled viciously. "Well, nonetheless, let's see what you've got." He turned his hand palm up and moved his fingers back and forth, motioning for her to attack. Molly didn't move.

"Are we just going to stare at each other?" Dunston asked, not expecting an answer. He waited for another ten seconds before he jumped toward her. Before landing, he drew his right arm back and extended his left. The moment his feet hit the ground he shifted all his forward momentum to his right fist. In one quick motion, the attacker switched the position of his arms and thrust his right fist toward Molly's chest.

With equal speed, she drew her right hand across her body and pushed his advancing arm off target. Her left arm swung in a counter-clockwise circle in front of her body and grabbed his extended arm. She twisted his limb and exposed the unprotected side of his body. Her right fist had a clear shot at his kidney, but as she drew back to punch, the target was gone.

Dunston kicked his right leg in the air, followed by his left, and broke free of Molly's grip in a spectacular cartwheel.

He landed directly in front of her, but she had no time to admire his acrobatics. An assortment of punches, blocks, kicks, and turns filled Molly's head as she analyzed her opponent's new position. In the half a second she had to decide, she picked "down." As she dropped to a squat, Dunston's left leg passed over her head.

Without a moment of thought, she brought her hands to the ground and used them as feet. Her legs extended out in front of her. In the blink of an eye, she spread them open like a pair of scissors. She caught her assailant's recoiling left leg and forced it off balance past his right leg. The result sent Dunston the ground with a thud.

Not wasting time appreciating her fancy footwork, Molly returned her feet to the ground. She raised her arms in the air, swinging them like windmills in two circles as she sprung with her feet. The result propelled her body through the air backwards, landing her perfectly on her feet. Instinctively she resumed her defensive stance.

Dunston stood up slowly and dusted off his shirt. "I'm impressed," he sarcastically applauded her as he too moved into a similar pose. "That wasn't learned at the Academy, was it?"

She again refused to answer.

"You seem very well disciplined," he praised her, bringing his hand to the corner of his lip. "I underestimated you," he added as he looked at the blood on the tips of his fingers. "Let's not have that happen again."

Dunston, like lightning, struck first to start the next series of attacks.

Molly was equally prepared for each of his punches and kicks. She answered his every move with a block or kick of her own. The two moved throughout the room exchanging well-timed and well-executed moves. As they continued to square off for nearly ten minutes, Molly found herself beginning to feel winded. Dunston, on the other hand, looked as fresh as he did at the start. Molly began to realize that unless she leveled a serious blow to him, it would end in her defeat.

However, that opportunity was never going to present itself. Dunston's eyes caught a glimpse of one of the monitors in the room and realized this melee had to end. As Molly came on him in a roundhouse kick, he grabbed the back of a sturdy desk chair and propelled it at her advancing body. The impact with the chair sent Molly cascading across the room and abruptly smashed into a wall. Her body stopped all movement as her arms and legs fell to the floor and were still.

Dunston stood in middle of the room perplexed. Two things had happened in the last ten minutes he had no answers for, and he needed explanations quickly. Tired from his fight with Molly, he walked to the screen that caught his attention. He slammed his fist to the desktop, causing the items on top to jump.

"SHERMAN!" he yelled. "Show me the current weather map for the Boston area."

"*The current Boston weather is displayed on the screen in front of you.*"

The image had not changed. It continued to show the Boston area, the entire state of Massachusetts for that matter, completely void of any foul weather.

Dunston turned around and looked at the back of the head across the room. Matt continued to type away at the keyboard in front of him. "SHERMAN, who's in the building?"

"Presently there are four people, all in this room."

Dunston, realizing the situation was swinging farther and farther from his control, asked, "Who is in this room, SHERMAN?"

"*You, Ralph Samson, an unknown person, and Matthew Malone.*"

"Matthew Malone," Dunston repeated.

Matt pressed the keyboard four last times and turned in the chair to face Raymond Dunston.

"You're Matthew Malone?"

Matt's nod slowed down as he spotted Molly on the floor. She slowly sat up, holding an arm that was bent in an odd direction.

"I tried," she said, the look of pain on her face. Matt was unsure if the look was for the defeat or the apparent broken arm.

"What are you doing here?" Dunston asked as if he felt concern for the young boy.

"I'm saving my school and putting an end to this game you're playing."

"You attend Wesley-Hampton Academy?" he asked as his mind raced.

"I do now."

Dunston shook his head. "That can't be. You're supposed to be in a foster home. I made sure of it. I left you with Harriet Helmut." He stared at Matt for a moment. "How did you get out?"

Matt returned the stare, wondering what was going on behind those steel gray eyes. How did he know who he was and where he lived? What did he mean by "I made sure of it?" Matt was preparing his answer, but Dunston beat him to it.

"Douglas McMichael! That's how. Why can't he leave well enough alone?"

"Well, I'm glad he took me from that lousy place. And now I get to ruin your plans." Matt turned back to the computer keyboard and prepared to press the enter key.

"I knew your Mother, Matthew. Did you know that?"

Matt's finger froze in midair over the key. He turned the chair back toward Dunston. "How?"

Dunston smiled. "She was my wife."

Matt listened, but lingered over the words and how they evolved in his brain. He looked up from his thoughts. "That …"

Dunston quickly put his hand up to stop him. "No, no. She was your mother, but I am not your father. She was having an affair. DNA testing proved all three points."

The facts came faster than Matt could handle them.

Howell, MR.   Wesley-Hampton Academy

"We met at Wesley-Hampton Academy where she and her father were on a team of engineers that build the computer."

"You killed her!" Matt shouted. "You killed her!" Without another thought, he spun around and faced the keyboard again. This time nothing stopped his finger from pressing the key.

A rumble began and the entire building shuttered as it had done earlier. Dunston helplessly watched as his control center trembled and a horrified look found his face.

"What have you done?" Dunston yelled, rushing up to Matt's chair.

With a cold, hard stare, Matt turned slowly around as the rumbling decreased. He stood up from his chair and pointed to the monitor across the room.

Dunston turned and took in the information it revealed. The area around Boston was as clear as ever, but the sight north of Dallas told a different story. Dark masses circled a small spot, causing it to look like an island.

At first Dunston directed his question at Matt. "What did..." and decided to instead ask the computer. "SHERMAN, why did the storm change?"

"*I was programmed to change it.*"

"By who?"

"*By Matthew Malone.*"

Dunston's look went from puzzled to irritated and back again. "Who gave him authorization?"

"*You did.*"

He stood there stunned. His diabolical mind reeled through the event of the last hour. There was nothing he had said or done to give the computer instructions for granting anyone control. All he could manage to say was, "But how?"

"With this," Matt said, holding up his SPA. "Sherman's Personal Assistant—quite handy."

Dunston stared at the device in Matt's outstretched hand. The pieces to the puzzle were there, but he was having a difficult time getting them to fit.

"The same code the Wesley-Hampton computer uses for user information is the same one SHERMAN uses. When I asked SHERMAN to download to my SPA, it recognized the code and I was added to the control hierarchy," Matt explained.

With a glance at the map, Dunston realized the circle of storms was closing. "SHERMAN, stop the storm!"

"*I can not.*" There was moment of silence.

"There's little you can do," Matt stated matter-of-factly. "I've locked you out from most of the commands. SHERMAN now belongs to me!"

"You little..." Dunston never finished his last sentence, nor did he continue moving malevolently toward Matt. He never realized where the kick had come from, but Matt saw it all.

Matt watched as Molly quietly stood up, clutching her twisted arm across her chest. He made certain that all of Dunston's attention was on him and that Molly was given the chance she needed to continue what she started.

Like a cat, she gingerly moved into position, waiting for an excellent opportunity. When she realized Dunston was completely absorbed in the events, she struck.

Holding her arm tight to the point of severe pain, she charged him. With all her strength, she performed a powerful roundhouse kick that sent her former assailant flying sideways into a rack of crates. The metal rack and all its contents, as if irritated, tumbled down on top of the intruding body. Dunston lay motionless under a mound of crates and shelves.

"First rule of engagement: never turn your back on your opponent," Molly laughed. Her feeling of joy was short-lived as reality took hold on the situation again. Her arm now hurt worse than before and the maps disclosed less unaffected area. The storm was closing in

"We're trapped," she said.

"No. There's one way out. We need to be quick."

Matt grabbed the chair he was using earlier and spun it around toward Molly. He instructed her to sit down and he would push her down the hall.

The two were leaving the room as SHERMAN said, "*The download is complete, Matthew. I cannot wait to meet my sister.*"

Molly shot him a contorted look. "What was that all about?"

"I found an open channel, for data only, out of the building and had SHERMAN download his entire memory core into SYLVIA's extra space."

"Why?"

"I'll show you why," Matt cryptically told her as they stopped at the door and grabbed Molly's shoes and socks. Then with a mighty push, Matt started the chair's momentum down the hall. As the chair's energy generated the necessary force to propel it easily down the hall, Molly began questioning Matt.

Matt told her what transpired while she was locked in battle. When they arrived at the control center, SHERMAN had already gotten the information from his SPA when it downloaded the map. By the time he sat down to the command screen, the computer had already cleared him of the passwords. He had all the power that Dunston had. And like Dunston, he had the power to remove people from control.

"The first thing I did was strip Dunston of power. Next, I contacted the others and unlocked their room. I told them to get out of the building as fast as they could. They were to head toward the vehicles. Once outside, their SPAs would work again.

"Conner took the others and left. He wanted to stay and help us, but I told him there was nothing they could do. Reluctantly they left. I told him to ignore anything they saw as far as weather. I would make sure they were out of harm's way."

Matt slowed down the speeding chair as he approached the doors he wanted.

"I commanded SHERMAN to pause the storm in Boston and relocate it. I then had the computer duplicate the storm into a total of four. I placed them around this building. The tornados that Dunston planned should be starting soon. Each storm had a total of four."

Molly looked wide-eyed at Matt, who was reaching for the door handle. "You mean to tell me there are sixteen tornadoes heading right for us?"

Matt pushed down the handle and held it there. "Yep. There's no way this building will survive."

"How are we getting out?"

Matt smiled and pulled open the door. He pushed Molly and the chair into the room and the lights flickered on.

Molly stared ahead and slowly stood up, still holding her arm tight. "Is that what I think it is?"

Matt nodded his head.

Chapter Eighteen
"Time to leave, in style."
– Matt Malone

Matt motioned for Molly to follow him as he headed for the vehicle in the center of the room. At first glance, it looked like a supped-up golf cart. It wasn't large; there was seating for only two people. The space normally left on the back for bags of golf clubs was completely closed in. The passenger compartment was not covered with the typical shade roof, but rather a clear dome made of polymer. All of these changes would have been enough to draw anyone's attention, but those things went unnoticed at first. What attracted Molly's attention first was the space below the tires. The entire cart was not resting on the ground, but rather floating a few inches above it.

"It's a hover car?"

"I found it in the data in SHERMAN. Isn't it incredible?"

Molly didn't know what to say. She was staring at something that her mind kept saying was impossible. *Cars cannot float on the air*, she reminded herself. Her eyes were hooked as she held her injured arm tight. It hurt, but she kept working to mentally block the pain. Over the last three years, she had fractured her ankle and broken two fingers. None of them hurt more than her arm did, but looking at this levitating car made her forget about the magnitude of nerves screaming along her shattered limb.

Matt helped her to the modified cart's door and guided her in. He closed the clear plastic door and raced to the other side. Once in his seat he studied the buttons and gauges. On the familiar side were a steering wheel, acceleration and brake pedal, and a speedometer. It was the electromagnetic-balance meter and the damper controls on the armrest on either side of the driver that caught his attention.

Molly read the look on his face as his eyes darted from familiar to unfamiliar and back again. "Do you know how to drive or fly this thing?"

The situation they were in called for a "Yes! Definitively." But Matt's awkward glance and scrunched forehead didn't even come close to a fraction of that assurance.

"I understand the basics," he told her, injecting as much confidence as he could. "I could do with some help starting it."

Letting her arm drop to her lap with a thud of pain, Molly reached out her fully intact arm and pressed a button labeled SHERMAN.

"SHERMAN, how do we start the hover car?"

Without a moment's pause the answer was given: *"Press the red button on the steering wheel."*

Matt found the button.

"If you want to switch between antigravity floatation and tires, press the orange button to the left of the start."

Throwing vanity aside, Matt asked, "SHERMAN, what should the electromagnetic-balance meter be at?"

"For normal driving conditions it should be around 50."

"What's normal?" Molly inquired.

"When the vehicle is moving at speeds under thirty mph."

"Does it have a top speed?" Matt asked, knowing speed would be essential.

"The fastest the hover cart has ever gone has been forty-five mph.   At that speed the electromagnetic-balance meter would read 95."

Not wanting to waste more time, Matt pressed the red button. The only indication the vehicle responded to the button was from a low humming noise they suddenly heard and that the vehicle raised slightly higher off the ground.

"SHERMAN, what do the damper controls do?" Matt asked.

"*They regulate the air entering the intakes at the side. This keeps the vehicle level. Are you planning to take this hover cart for a drive, Matthew?*" the computer asked in its southern drawl.

"Yes, SHERMAN. We are."

"*I need to advise against it, Matthew. The conditions outdoors have worsened. There are sixty mile per hour wind gusts and the conditions are right for tornados. You would have a very difficult time keeping the cart level.*"

Matt gave a hopeful look at Molly. "We don't have a choice. The conditions indoors are going to get equally bad. I think we'll stand a better chance outside."

"SHERMAN, what is the top speed on wheels?"

"*Much less. The top speed is eight mph.*"

"We would look like a slug trying to escape a fire," Matt equated. "I say we give it a try."

The two were wrenched from their conversation as a gust of wind blew hard at the aluminum doors in front of them. The twenty-foot high doors shook violently, nearly separating themselves from the wall.

Only a moment passed and the doors, thirty feet away, shook again.

"We've got to get out of here," they both yelled together over the growing winds.

Matt was in the middle of asking the computer to open the doors when a burst of air from outside complied. The left door swung viciously open, slamming itself into the connecting wall. The right door had little choice about staying hinged. It was ripped from its grip and thrown toward the little car.

Molly and Matt ducked as the massive metal panel sailed over the top of the domed vehicle, missing it by less than an inch. The cart shook side to side as the wind freely blew around the room. Crates on the rear wall tumbled to the ground in a stunning crash. One crate tumbled several times until it crashed into an open barrel of garbage, and the rubbish spewed across the floor.

The wind playfully grabbed the debris and sent it flying in all directions. From the pile, a whirlpool erupted. A tiny tornado of trash and wind spun freely and then died.

Matt's eyes leaped from the small vortex to the open door. He slammed his foot on the acceleration pedal and the vehicle exploded forward. Matt and

Molly were pushed backward into their seats by the force of momentum. The little car tore across the room and burst from the building.

The two sites were incredible. The white cart with the plastic dome and its two astonished passengers soaring above the ground and the growing storm they drove directly into. The two travelers viewed the storm, equally amazed, as they found themselves as players in a most extraordinary display of weather.

The sky darkened near completely. Rain speckled on the dome above them. Then without warning, they were pelted with a burst of hail. Small, round, frozen balls bounced off the charging vehicle. Matt pointed to the grove of trees where they left the bikes. Four of the bikes were gone and the trees bent toward them, pointing their upper branches at them as if saying, "Look at the strange car."

Matt felt the wind whip under the small cart as it teetered back and forth. He fingered the joystick control on the left armrest and the cart leveled for a moment. He could feel it lean to the left as Molly's shoulder pressed into his. Using the right damper controls, he was able to level the car again.

Between damper adjustments, Matt also steered around moving and stationary objects.

He kept his eyes glued to the view in front of them, even when Molly yelled, "Look at that! There must be at least six funnels over that way."

Matt didn't need to look to their left to see any funnels forming. Straight ahead, he watched two come alive.

As the vehicle wavered to the right, Matt caught sight of at least four more vortexes, much larger than the two before them. He fought to right the hovering cart. The converging winds made it very difficult, but he was able to manage.

He could hear Molly wince in pain as the jostling caused her arm to flop about freely every time her good arm grabbed for something to steady herself. Even with the seatbelt on, she was thrown like a rag doll.

Matt decided their best chance was straight ahead. The thought of two small tornados looked better than the thought of the multitude of larger ones on either side. He fought to steady the craft as he headed for the space between the advancing pair.

Molly continued to watch the storm around them grow stronger every moment. The fascination ended when a large tree branch slammed into the top of the plastic dome. Both Molly and Matt wondered how strong the dome might be and shared their concern with a glance at each other.

Matt returned his stare on the two small whirlwinds ahead of them. As they grew closer, the distance between them grew larger. This was the comforting part; the unnerving part was what the winds were doing to the vehicle. The nearer they got the more control the wind was taking from Matt.

"Are we going to make it?" Molly asked with an abundance of trepidation in her voice.

"If we don't, I don't want to hear about my bad driving!" Matt answered jokingly, trying to ease the tension.

Any stress that was relieved by his last comment quickly returned tenfold. A gust of wind hit the driver's side of the car like a rampaging bull. While Matt moved the dampener controls in order to compensate, another bull slammed into Molly's side.

The little car was tossed, wobbling, into the air. Then, without warning, was slammed down on the ground. Matt felt the immobile tires drag and scrape across the rocky earth until the vehicle could regain it gravitational advantage.

The two tornados were nearly upon them. They were, Matt guessed, at least 100 yards apart. He hoped it would be enough.

The two watched the whirling winds toss objects around in rotating directions.

"Matt," Molly said serenely, "those two funnels are closing in on each other. Do you think this is a good idea?"

"I think it's our only idea, Molly. If we turn around now, any places to escape will be gone. Each of these funnels is heading for one spot: the building."

Additional conversation never occurred. It was replaced by screams of fear and pain as the winds attacked the car from every angle. First, it spun completely around as it was again lifted into the air. Pointing toward the original bearings and at least twenty feet in the air, it began to rotate. Like a bullet making its way down the long barrel of a rifle, the small car twisted and gained velocity as it was sucked forward.

Molly held tight her broken arm and surrendered herself to the tumbling car. She watched with dreadfulness as the horrific view ahead of them changed from upright to upside down and back again. She shut her eyes to avoid the dizziness that crept into her skull.

Matt abandoned his struggle with the controls. They were unresponsive in this insane spinning. He could hear objects he could not see crash into the side of the propelling cart.

From outside of the car the view was amazing as the white, rotating, and impassive car was magnetically drawn toward the two tornados that were now only fifty feet apart.

The two passengers didn't have the luxury of this view; in fact, they had no view at all. The rotating increased, causing the blood in their bodies to gather farther from their brains and as the screams died, they passed out.

Chapter Nineteen
"I have the best little brother!"
– SYLVIA

All around, everything was silent. Matt slowly allowed the world to return to his brain as he cautiously sat up right. He had found himself lying on his back in unfamiliar surroundings. Everything for the past week had been unfamiliar surroundings, he mused, as objects began to come into focus. The cabinets, the countertops, the gurneys all added up to a hospital.

Insistent pounding on his temple caused him to raise his right hand to his forehead. The feeling of gauze and tape met his fingertips. Sliding his hand around his head, he traced the bandage all the way around.

This brought on a broader scan of his entire body. Matt moved his hands down his face and discovered bandages covering small spots on his cheeks and neck. He looked down his left arm and found his hand wrapped in dressing. His fingers poked out the ends and he could painlessly wiggle them.

"Ah," came a voice across the room, followed by a nurse in a white dress that complimented her dark skin and hair. "My patient is alive."

Matt watched her move closer. He had never seen her before and realized he had no idea where he was. What hospital was this? Was he still in Texas?

"How are you feeling?" she asked, not expecting an answer. "My name is Carol. Nurse Carol, everyone calls me."

She smiled a disarming smile and Matt caught the nametag pinned to her dress. In bold red letters it read "CAROL" and below her name Matt saw "Wesley-Hampton Academy."

"Am I back at the school?"

"Yep!" she joyfully replied, pushing the sensor end of her temperature probe under his tongue. "Got in here two days ago. You and your friend were pretty beat up."

Matt tried to ask about Molly but the thermometer protruding from his mouth garbled the words. He waited impatiently for the beep that would instruct Carol to remove the impediment.

The moment she removed it he spit the question out. "Where's Molly?"

Carol looked at the end of the thermometer's digital readout and recorded her findings on a clipboard. "She'll be right back, dear. Jeffery took her down for another x-ray."

Any question Matt wanted to ask was about to be answered. He looked toward the double doors that parted open and he saw a table being pushed in the room. Molly lay asleep on top. Her cast arm rested on her sleeping chest. Matt could see the bandages and gauze spewed across her body as well.

Jeffery guided the gurney parallel with Matt's and walked away. Matt stared at the sleeping redhead. Questions ran through his mind in the form of bewilderments. *What happened two days ago? How did we survive? Did we put an end to Dunston?*

Almost on cue, Matt looked from Molly to the opening doors. Mr. McMichael entered the room and Matt suddenly felt a sense of relief. He was now going to get answers.

The headmaster rolled his chair to Molly. He paused a moment and turned to Matt. He rolled to his side between the two youths. "I'm beginning to think the two of you are indestructible."

Matt smiled, not knowing how to respond.

"There are several who want to talk to you. Are you up to it?"

Matt's team raced to the forefront of his mind and he nodded his head. He watched Mr. McMichael press a button on the armrest of his chair.

A familiar English voice spoke to him. *"Hello, Mathew. It's good to see you back."*

"Hello, SYLVIA. Are you okay?"

"Never better." A pause followed. Matt waited, confused. Of all the people he wanted to see, SYLVIA was not anywhere near the top half of the list. *"I want to thank you for what you did two days ago. If it was not for your intuitive and ingenuous planning, I never would have met my little brother."*

For the second time in as many minutes, Matt wasn't sure he knew what to say.

"SHERMAN shared with me all about what you did. And you even had the wherewithal to transfer all his knowledge to my memory banks. Incredible!"

"Did everything download?"

"Oh, yes. Mr. St. Lucia has been up around the clock going through everything. He told me I would be able to take advantage of several upgrades."

"He's been running around the entire lab ever since the first data stream began to arrive," Mr. McMichael acknowledged. "Some of the information is incredible, but you already knew that."

"It was my brother that alerted us to your whereabouts. He saved your lives."

"You flew passed the two tornados with unbelievable speed. Once you passed their threat, the skies cleared and sun was out. The car you were in tried to right itself, but failed. It was SYLVIA who intervened and brought you down to the ground. Rather hard, I might add."

"What happened to the lab?"

"It was completely destroyed. Actually, the first couple of category 5 tornados that made impact ripped the building apart. The rest was overkill. I think you could have used a little less force," Mr. McMichael said with a smile.

Matt smiled back and felt his cheeks get warm. "Was there any sign of Dunston?"

Mr. McMicheal's tone got serious again. "We sent a team into investigate. There was no sign of anybody, dead or alive."

"He got away?"

Mr. McMichael shook his head slowly. "We don't know."

A quiet lull entered the conversation and Matt found himself looking over to Molly. He felt a hand rest on his arm.

"Matt, I was very impressed with the strength of character you exhibited. Under extreme pressure you kept your wits about you. I'm very proud of you."

A surge of emotion sailed through Matt's body, and a churning began in his stomach as he listened to the words. When Matt's green eyes locked on the blue eyes that were looking him over, he blushed. No one ever spoke to him that way.

"Mr. McMichael, when I was at the lab, Dunston told me he knew my mother. Was that true?" he asked those compassionate eyes with complete sincerity.

Mr. McMichael rubbed his hand on his cheek and slowly began his answer. "Yes, it is true. When Raymond Dunston was here he married your mother, but …"

"I already know. He's not my father," Matt finished the sentence for him. "Do you know who my father was?"

The headmaster stared at the inquisitive boy for a moment. Matt could read nothing from his stone cold face. "No, I don't," he finally said. "Your mother was a very private person and kept a great deal to herself."

Matt continued to stare until his eyes grew heavy and they slowly looked to the floor. It wasn't the answer he wanted.

With a desperate urge to change the conversation, he asked, raising his look again, "How's the team?"

"They're doing well and very grateful for saving their lives." He patted Matt on the leg and rolled his chair away from the bed. "I'll send them in."

Matt watched the wheelchair roll from the room. A couple of minutes passed and the door slid open again. Nurse Carol led the team members into the room. They all walked up to Matt's bed.

"Did you hear what I said? No more than five minutes," Nurse Carol instructed them sternly. "He needs to rest."

No one spoke until Carol was out of earshot.

"I don't need rest," Matt told them.

"Oh, the old bat needs to do something," Doug said, receiving Julie's elbow in his side.

"She's nice! Leave her alone!" Julie playfully reproached Doug.

"That's because you're always in here getting mended. And she brings you ice cream," Doug teased. "She never treats me that way."

"No wonder!" Julie shot back and then turned to Matt with a smile. "Well, did you like it?"

Matt's face took on a confused look, and Conner cleared things up. "She's talking about your first assignment."

"Parts of it were fun"

There was a low groan behind them and they all turned around. Molly was trying to sit up but was having a difficult time with only one working arm. "Can't a girl get any sleep around here?"

"We're sorry, Molly. We didn't mean to wake you," Beth said for the entire group.

"Don't be. Do you think I like lying here all day?" She finally pushed herself up to a sitting position. "That nurse would keep us in here until sometime next year, if she had her way."

Doug passed an "I-told-you-so" glance at Julie. She ignored him.

The teamed talked for nearly ten minutes. It finally took two attempts from Nurse Carol to get the visitors to leave.   The room fell quiet with the conversations gone. While the nurse gave Molly her medicines, Matt checked his e-mail on his SPA that Conner had brought. There was one from Joey.

Dear Matt,

I have some great news. I'm not staying at the foster home anymore. I've moved in with the Hathaways. That's the name of the family. They're really nice. I have a room all to myself.

If everything goes well, I hope they will adopt me. I'll start school at Haven-Summit

Elementary School on Monday. There are some very smart kids there, but none as smart as you. I hope your new school is going well. I'm sure you're the best in your class.

Well, I have to go. We're heading to the zoo and the beach today.

Your friend,
Joey

P.S. Please write me back.

P.S.S. The raining at our old foster home finally stopped, just as fast as it started. Sometimes I wish I could control the weather, don't you?

Matt reread the last P.S.S. and laughed.

Chapter Twenty
"I'm home at last."
– Matthew Malone

Matt lowered the SPA. He felt great for Joey and the chance Joey had for getting a family. He admitted to himself how wonderful it would be to have a family. The thought of his mother entered his head. What was she like? Who was his father? Was he still alive? With all the power Mr. McMichael had, could he find out who he was?

The rest of the day Molly and Matt talked about the events they could remember. In the early afternoon, the team made another visit. It would be their last, since Nurse Carol told them they would be able to join the rest of the school at dinner.

Mr. Hampton stopped in and handed them both a copy of their class schedule. They were expected to be in class in the morning. He complemented them on a job well done. He told them he had never, in all his years, witnessed two students take on so much in their first week.

"If this week was any indication of what you two are capable of, it's going to be fun watching you in action," he predicted with a big smile.

By late afternoon, most of the staff had been in to see them. The compliments seemed to go on forever. Even Nurse Carol praised them while they changed into their school clothes behind curtains. She walked them as far as the cafeteria hallway. They thanked her and made their way alone.

When the two students entered the large dining hall, all conversation stopped. Everybody turned to look at the two green-shirted students. Then the room erupted in tumultuous applause. Chairs slid backwards as student after student took their clapping to their feet.

Matt and Molly stopped at the entrance. Nothing in their past could compare to the warm and accepted feeling that cruised through their veins.

Slowly they began walking again toward the green tables. The applause continued until Mr. McMicheal's voice was heard over the PA system asking everyone to take a seat.

"I think the feeling is obvious and unanimous in this room. We owe not only our school's survival to your cunningness, but our very lives."

The students instantly returned to their applause.

The two sat down with their teammates, who were loudly clapping with the entire school.

The ovation continued for quite a long time and Matt found himself drifting along with it. He felt a rush of genuine affection and realized he, like Joey, had found his home, his family.

Howell, MR.   Wesley-Hampton Academy

www.ingramcontent.com/pod-product-compliance
Lightning Source LLC
Chambersburg PA
CBHW031913190626
46814CB00003BA/1264